HARMONY

HARMONY

STEEL BROTHERS SAGA
BOOK TWENTY-NINE

HELEN HARDT

WATERHOUSE PRESS

To all Steel fans...

Thank you for hanging in there with me through Book 29!

PROLOGUE

Brianna

"It's Dragon," Jesse says, his voice low, slightly shaking.

"What happened?" Maddie asks.

"I don't know. He may have OD'd on something. I'll keep you all posted as well as I can."

I reach out to touch Jesse's arm, but he yanks it away.

I'm hurt, but we had this chat.

No distractions.

And this—whatever just happened to Dragon—is a major distraction. Jesse doesn't need me on top of that.

The elevator doors close, and Maddie clasps her hand to her mouth. "Is Dragon going to make it?"

"God, I hope so." My heart is racing.

"What are they going to do for a drummer?"

"I don't know. Brock used to play the drums. He and David and a couple other guys had a garage band."

"Were they any good?"

"Hell no. They sucked."

"Then how is that going to do us any good?"

I shake my head. "I don't know, Mads. But Brock may be all we have."

"Maybe Dragon's okay. Maybe he's just drunk or something."

"God, I hope so," I say again.

I stand against the wall, trying not to hyperventilate. I don't know Dragon well. No one does, really.

Except Jesse. I've spotted him and Dragon alone and talking many times—mainly because I'm always watching Jesse. The two of them seem to be close friends.

This must be killing Jesse.

"It's eight thirty," Maddie says. "We're supposed to meet Brock, Callie, and Donny for sightseeing in half an hour."

"Right. I guess I forgot to set my alarm."

"Me too. I was so angry after Jesse broke up that date—or whatever it was—with Zane that I came up here and pouted. None of that seems important now."

"No, it's not important. In fact, it never was. We should be thanking your brother, Maddie, and we've got to fix this for him."

"How are we supposed to fix this? We can't go back in time and make sure Dragon stays away from whatever he took."

"No. But we can find a drummer. What floor is Emerald Phoenix on?"

"What are you suggesting?"

"We have no choice. We have to see if their drummer can fill in for Dragon."

"Emerald Phoenix's drummer is not going to fill in for Dragon," Maddie says. "He has his own band."

I sigh. Maddie's right. "Then Brock is their only choice."

"If they have to cancel this tour... Jesse and Rory are going to be so disappointed. This tour could have meant their careers, and it meant so much to our family."

"I understand more than you know. I'm going to fix this, Maddie. If it's the last thing I do, I'm going to fix this for your brother."

CHAPTER ONE

Jesse

Emergency rooms in the UK apparently aren't called emergency rooms. They're called A&E, or the accident and emergency department, part of the National Health Service hospitals. They also don't require any up-front payment.

Still, someone—I'm so hazy I couldn't pick him or her out of a lineup—hands me a clipboard of paperwork to fill out for Dragon.

And it hits me—how very little I know about him. I know his age but not his date of birth. I know his first name and his last name. I'm not even sure of his address. I know where he lives, but I never think about the number on the house where he rents a room.

But one thing I *can* state as fact.

He's had a drug problem in the past, and he's been through rehab at least once.

I fill in as much information as I can, and then I take the clipboard back to the clerk on duty. "I'm sorry. This is all I have. We're from the United States."

"Good enough, then." She takes it from me and wrinkles her brow. "Dragon?"

"That's his name. He claims it's on his birth certificate, though I have to admit I've never seen it."

"Do you have his passport, dear?"

His passport. That would help. "It's probably back in the hotel room. I wasn't exactly thinking about grabbing it when he was passed out cold."

"Not a problem." She flips through the papers on the clipboard. "We'll get all the information eventually. Go ahead and have a seat. The doctors will keep you updated."

"Thank you."

I turn, but her voice interrupts me once more.

"Sorry. What's your relationship to the patient?"

I shrug. "Friend. Roommate."

She cocks her head, and for the first time I notice she's gray-haired with blue eyes. "He's your roommate, and you don't know his address?"

"Sorry." My vision blurs for a second, and I blink to refocus. "I meant roommate here, in London. Not at home. I wrote the name of our hotel on the form, but again, I don't know the address. I could look it up for you."

"You don't need to do that. Very good, then." She removes the papers from the clipboard and begins tapping on her computer.

Apparently that means I'm done this time.

I'm not even sure what time it is.

I pull out my phone and check. Still morning. I haven't had any breakfast, but I can't eat.

I have two texts—one from Maddie and one from Brianna, both asking how Dragon is.

Another text pops up, this one from Cage asking the same thing.

I don't know what to say.

I start a group text with all of them. I don't want to have to be typing shit five different times.

My group text includes Maddie, Brianna, Cage, Jake, Rory, and Callie. I don't know Brock's and Donny's phone numbers, and I only know Brianna's because she texted me.

> *No news yet. He's in the back with the doctors.*

Then I text Cage only.

> *We need a drummer for tonight. Get on that. Please.*

I shove my phone back in my pocket and glance at the display of magazines on the table next to my chair. Nothing looks the least bit interesting, and it's not like I could focus on anything other than Dragon. I take one anyway—*Time Out London*. To my surprise, the cover story is on the current Emerald Phoenix tour through the UK. I shuffle through the pages and find the article. Dragonlock isn't mentioned. Why would we be? First, we're nobodies compared to Emerald Phoenix, and second, we were a last-minute replacement when the previous opener dropped out.

Great. Like I need a reminder of this tour and everything that's at stake.

I shove the magazine back onto the table. This is all my fault. I should've stayed with Dragon last night. I should've given those women the boot.

I know Dragon. He's worked so hard at his sobriety. He wouldn't have taken anything hard on his own.

He may have smoked a little weed—but only if the women

brought it. Recreational marijuana is still illegal in the UK. He probably drank a few beers. He tends to stay away from the hard stuff.

But no matter how horny or drunk he got, he would not have ingested anything hard. He would not have risked his sobriety—not for anything, and certainly not for a couple of groupies.

Not with this tour at stake.

Those two girls...

What were their names again? Jenny and Andrea? They were both brunettes, but other than that, I can't remember anything unique about either of them. I have no last names, no other identifying characteristics. At this point, Dragon probably won't be able to remember anything about them either.

I'm almost positive they slipped him something. Some narcotic, maybe. Heroine or fentanyl. Or maybe something to produce amnesia like roofies or ketamine.

No, probably not one of those. Neither of those would have knocked him out. They just would have caused amnesia. Oh hell, I don't even know. I know nothing about drugs. I could take out my phone, do a quick search of all the illicit drugs that have the possibility of rendering a person unconscious, but frankly, I don't want to know. Besides, for everything you find on the internet, there's another source that will tell you it's wrong.

I just have to wait. When Dragon's toxicology report comes back, I'll know for sure what's in his system.

I don't even care what it is at this point. I just want them to save his life.

Even if they do, he won't be in any condition to perform

tonight. We'll have to find another drummer. I've got Cage on that now. Between him, Jake, and Rory... I hope they can come up with something.

I'm in a foreign country, and I don't know anyone. I certainly don't know any drummers, though I'm sure they're plentiful.

Still, Dragon is a freaking genius on percussion. No one will be able to fill his shoes.

We're fucked.

We can't perform without a drummer.

Which means we can't perform.

My phone buzzes. Rory.

"Hey, Ror."

"No news yet?"

"Not yet." I glance at the door they dragged Dragon through. "It hasn't been that long."

"Look. I've been talking to the guys. We all hate what happened, but we think we may have a solution."

"Oh?" I know better than to let myself feel hopeful...yet a spark of hope surges into me.

"You know Jake plays drums."

"Yeah, that's right. I forgot about that."

"So he could take over for Dragon, but that means..."

I draw in a breath. "That means I have to go back on lead guitar."

"Yeah."

"And taking me off guitar to concentrate on vocals is what drew Emerald Phoenix to us," I say, more to myself than to Rory.

"Yes, but surely they'd understand—"

"They won't understand, Rory. They're not going to

understand that one of our band members OD'd, and we're screwed."

"Jess, this tour means everything."

I scoff. "You think you have to tell me that?"

"I'm just saying that it *is* a solution. Is it the perfect solution? No, of course not. The perfect solution would be for Dragon to be playing the drums. But that isn't going to happen." Her voice starts to break. "This is all my fault."

"Your fault?" I can't help another scoff. "Rory, for God's sake. How the hell is this your fault?"

"I got you your own room, Jesse. If I hadn't..."

I see where her mind is going. If she hadn't, I would have been in the room last night with Dragon, and I would've kept this from happening.

She's right.

And that *is* where I should've been.

But it's not Rory's fault. It's mine.

Mine. I let myself get distracted.

Distracted by Brianna Steel.

I can't tell Rory that, though. But I can't let her blame herself either.

"You were thinking of the band when you got me that room, Ror. You knew I needed to sleep. And I did."

"I know. But if you had been with Dragon—"

"Stop right there. Dragon is a grown man. You think I could've stopped him from doing something he had his mind set on?"

I don't expect her to answer because we both know that the answer is yes. I *could* have stopped Dragon from taking drugs. I also think Dragon could have stopped *himself* from taking drugs.

"Rory," I say. "I don't know exactly what happened, but I'm almost positive that Dragon was drugged against his will. He knows how important this tour is. He wouldn't have risked it for anything."

"So you think it was one of those two little skanks, then?"

Rory's use of the word *skanks* surprises me. She's always the first to yell at anyone for slut shaming, and usually I agree with her. Right now, though? I hate those two for doing this to Dragon. If I could pick them out of a lineup, I'd have the cops after their firm little asses.

"I'd put money on it." I rise, pace across the waiting room. "Damn. I should've been there."

"I know. I shouldn't have gotten you that room."

I tug at my hair. "No, Rory. No, no, no. That's not what I'm saying. That's not what I'm saying at all."

"I know it's not, but I feel responsible." Rory lets out a soft sob. "What was I thinking?"

"You were thinking I needed to sleep. You made sure I did, and I thank you for that. I'm the one who should've been taking care of Dragon. This band is *my* responsibility."

"I won't let you do that to yourself, Jess. We are *all* responsible for this band, including Dragon."

"I know. I know. I just don't think he did this, Rory. I guess we won't know until he wakes up." I run my fingers through my hair. "*If* he fucking wakes up."

"Come on, Jesse. You can't think like that. He's going to be okay."

My heartbeat begins to accelerate, and it's already racing. I can't keep talking about this. I need to focus. "I've got to go."

"All right. Keep us posted. In the meantime, I think Jake is our only chance."

"I'll think about it."

I end the call. So we have Jake on drums, me on guitar. Cage on keyboard, and Rory singing. We'd still have four people onstage, and I could still sing. But Jett Draconis was right. When I'm focusing solely on singing with Rory, I'm better. Sure, I can still rock the place when I'm playing guitar and singing, but Rory and I together on vocals and nothing else... We make magic.

And we need that magic to make this tour a success.

We also need Dragon.

Dragon...

Man, he's had a rough life. He's conquered so much, overcome so many demons.

He can't go out like this. He just can't.

How long has it been?

Time seems to have suspended itself. Sometimes it seems like hours and hours have passed, and sometimes it seems like the ambulance pulled up to this hospital only seconds ago.

My heart is still pounding, and my stomach is churning. Nausea is creeping up my throat. Eating something would probably help, but the thought of putting anything in my mouth makes me want to upchuck.

Because I know the truth.

This *isn't* Rory's fault.

Hell, I don't even think it's Dragon's fault. I think he was probably drugged by those two little shitheads.

No. Only one person is at fault here.

The person who should've been taking care of the band instead of screwing Brianna Steel last night.

I had one big shot.

And I fucking blew it.

CHAPTER TWO

Brianna

Maddie and I are sitting with Rory, Brock, Donny, and Callie. Our server brought us each a breakfast of eggs, bacon, two types of sausage, potatoes, and roasted tomatoes, but not one of us has touched any of it.

The best I can do is sip the shitty cup of coffee I ordered. From now on I'll be drinking tea, even at breakfast. Coffee is not an English thing. I'm a coffee snob. My mother raised us only on the best, strongest, most robust coffee. A morning without coffee is foreign to me, but the English do tea like no one else. Their tea is a hundred times better than their coffee.

Why I'm thinking about coffee, I have no idea. A man's life—and the band's future—is at stake.

"You really think I should?" Rory asks.

What are they talking about? I've only been listening with one ear, and all the noises sound like they're coming through water, as if my ears are clogged. All I can think about is Jesse. Jesse, and how his big chance may have been ruined.

We had a big talk about distractions last night.

I was determined *not* to be one.

But in reality? It may be too late for that. Because if he hadn't been with me last night...

No. That wouldn't have mattered. He would've been in his

own room. He had his own room.

But still...

I can't help feeling a huge amount of guilt.

The conversation around me keeps going on. Should Rory do something? She doesn't feel right. *Right about what?* Maddie and Callie keep asking her what they can do for her, and she keeps saying nothing, that it's not their problem. It's hers. Then they move on to something else, and I stop listening again.

Until—

"I'm not sure you have a choice, babe." Brock's voice.

Rory crosses her arms and looks around the table. "I suppose I don't. We owe them an explanation. Excuse me for a minute." She scoots her chair away from the table, rises, and pulls out her phone as she walks away.

"You okay, sis?"

I widen my eyes at my brother's voice. "Yeah. I suppose."

Donny cocks his head. "You look kind of...out of it."

"What's going on? Who is Rory calling?"

"She's calling Heather Myles, Jett's wife. They exchanged phone numbers after the concert in Snow Creek, and they've kept in touch. She has to let Jett know what's going on with Dragon."

"You think they'll be angry?"

"I don't know, sis. I don't know these people very well."

"They're good people," Brock says. "Rory and I spent quite a bit of time with them. They'll be understanding, I'm sure, but they may decide that Dragonlock can't go on tonight."

I gasp. "Why would they decide *that*?"

"Because the contract is with Dragonlock, all five members of the band," Donny, the lawyer, says. "If all five can't go on, they'll be considered in breach."

My heart plummets to my stomach. This was their big chance. Jesse's big chance.

My heart aches for him. "What if they get a substitute drummer?"

"Where would we get a substitute drummer?" Brock asks.

I stare at him, forcing him to meet my gaze. "You."

Brock's eyebrows nearly fly off his forehead. "Me?"

"Yeah, you. You and Dave and those guys had that garage band back in middle school."

"Uh...in case you've forgotten, Bree, we were shitty."

"Still, you were the drummer, Brock."

"There's a reason I haven't played drums for ten years." Brock shakes his head. "I'm not an option, Bree. Believe me, I wish I were."

Rory returns to the table. "Heather and Jett are coming down. I need you to come with me, Brock. Since Jesse's not here, I guess I'm speaking for the band."

"Did you text Cage and Jake?" Brock asks.

"Yeah. They're coming down as soon as they can. Jake's looking over the percussion arrangements."

Brock nods, and the two of them walk away from the table. I don't know where they're meeting Jett and Heather, but of course they need to speak alone.

"I wish there were something I could do," Maddie says.

"We have to fix this," I say. "We just have to."

"I agree with you, Brianna," Callie says. "This means everything to my brother and sister, but how do we fix it?"

"I don't know." I shake my head. "I just don't know. I feel like there's something we could be doing. Something we should be seeing that we're not seeing."

"Rory and the guys figured out a way to make it happen.

Jesse's going to have to go back on guitar, and Jake will take over on drums." Donny takes a sip of his coffee and then nearly spits it out. "Man, this is terrible."

"Tea from now on," I say absently.

"As long as we're in the UK, no more coffee," my brother agrees.

"I suppose it's good that they're just the opening band," Maddie says. "I mean, if they can't play, they just won't. There won't be an opener."

Did those words just come out of Maddie's mouth? Maddie, who's usually so empathetic? "Maddie, this means everything to your brother and sister."

"I know that, Bree. I'm trying to look on the bright side." She sighs. "Although, you're right. That's not any kind of bright side."

"You mean your motivational guru hasn't trained you to see the bright side in any situation?" I say sarcastically.

Maddie's jaw drops, and the bottoms of her eyes fill with tears.

And I feel like the lowest scum on the bottom of a criminal's shoe, throwing that in her face. "Maddie, I'm sorry."

She sniffles back her tears. "I'm sure we're all just stressed out."

"You're letting me off the hook way too easily," I say.

"I'm just tired of feeling like shit," she says. "I was so horrid to Jesse last night when he wouldn't let us go off with Zane."

Donny's eyes shoot open. "Excuse me?"

Jeez. No one needs my big brother going all *big brother* right now.

"It's a long story, Donny."

"Do I need to kick that motherfucker's ass?" Donny asks,

not nicely.

"No," I say. "Jesse took care of it. And I'm glad he did."

Donny furrows his brow. "I am too. I guess I owe him one."

"And he was right," Maddie says. "I don't know what I was thinking. But I was so mean to him last night. I feel like..."

"You didn't do this, Maddie," I say.

"I know that. Objectively, anyway. Just feel like I messed with his vibe, you know?"

I sigh. Maddie didn't mess with Jesse's vibe. I did. I kept him distracted. Distracted, when he should've had his mind focused on the band. Maybe specifically focused on Dragon. Maybe then...

Maybe then...none of this would be happening.

Donny is scowling at me, and I wish I could go back in time.

Back in time...

Maybe if I had gone back to bed with Jesse. Maybe if...

Donny eyes Maddie and me. "I don't have to lecture you two about indiscriminate sex, do I?"

I resist an eye roll. Right. My brother, the quintessential womanizer, wants to lecture me about indiscriminate sex. It might interest him to know I was a virgin until a few days ago, but I'm not about to spill that little secret.

"Maybe I need to talk to you," Callie says straight to her little sister.

"My God, I feel bad enough as it is," Maddie says. "I was so angry with Jesse last night. How long were you down here with him after I left, Bree?"

All gazes fall on me then. Right. I was down here with him. I was the last person who saw him before he went to bed.

"Not for long," I say, trying to sound innocent.

"You were gone for a few hours," Maddie says, "before you came up to the room."

Donny and Callie both shoot daggers at me.

"What's she saying, sis?" Donny asks.

I blink. "We were down here talking. Jesse ordered a pizza, remember?"

Maddie nods. "That's right. He did order a pizza."

Nice. Saved by the pie we didn't stay to eat. I breathe in and force out the lie. "Right. So we ate pizza. Talked. Then we went our separate ways."

"Did he say anything about the two girls who went with Dragon to his room?"

"No, not really. Just that *he* wasn't into it, so he left Dragon to do his thing." I shake my head. "He must feel so terrible about that."

"I think we all feel pretty terrible," Callie says. "But Dragon is an adult. No one should have to babysit him."

I nod.

An adult.

That was the argument I gave my parents when I told them I was going on this trip. The argument I gave to Callie and Donny as well.

And how many times have I told Jesse I'm an adult? A grown-up?

Funny...

Being a grown-up doesn't really mean anything at all. You can still end up getting into lots of trouble.

I hope to God that Dragon is okay.

And even more than that? I hope Jesse isn't killing himself with guilt right now.

I really want to be the one to fix this for him.

CHAPTER THREE

Jesse

I stare into space.

People stroll by me—people of all looks and walks of life.

Two parents, worried about their screaming toddler, take a seat. They have to wait because my friend is unconscious.

They must wait and worry about their child—who may have a fever, may be sick. But the rules are ironclad. The child is conscious, so they have to wait.

I try to block out the sick child's screams. He can't be more than two or three, and his blond hair is slicked to his forehead with sweat. Most of the seats are filled in the waiting area, but except for the toddler, I can't tell who the patients are and who the family members and friends are. It's like they're stick people and they all look alike. They don't exist in my world because I don't know them. I don't care for them the way I care for Dragon. I don't appreciate their stories. All I know is that these plastic seats are damned uncomfortable on my ass.

The clerk who took Dragon's paperwork is busy, along with a nurse who seems to be assessing patients. The ER— or whatever the hell it's called here—is busy this morning, which is why the poor child can't be seen yet. He sits on his mother's lap, and she kisses his forehead, trying to soothe him. The father sits next to her, his face pale and lips twisted into a frown.

In the corner is a dedicated space for kids with toys and books, but no one plays there. The toddler is the only child here, and he's too sick to care. A vending machine sits next to the children's area. Again I think I should eat something, but I don't have any British change. It probably takes a credit card. Still, I don't move. I feel glued to this hard plastic chair.

Glued to this place.

Glued to misfortune. Glued to pennilessness. Glued to a fucked-up life.

Glued to—

"Stop it!" I say out loud.

Eyes dart toward me, but I don't care. I have to stop this train of thought because it's going to send me down a path I can't go. Not with Dragon's life and my career hanging in the balance.

Gratitude.

That's where I need to focus.

I'm here. I'm alive. I'm so damned grateful for everything I've received. To be on this tour.

It can't be over.

It can't be over this soon.

And it can't be over because of me.

"Mr. Locke?"

I jerk toward a voice. A woman wearing green scrubs, her blond hair pulled back into a ponytail, stands near the entrance to the waiting area.

"Who's here for Mr. Locke?"

I rise and walk toward her. "I am." My heart is stampeding against my chest. I can even see the movement if I look closely enough.

"And you are?" she asks.

"His friend. Roommate. My name is Jesse Pike."

"All right. I'm Dr. Nelson. Mr. Locke's toxicology screen came back positive."

My heart sinks to my stomach, though I'm not sure why. Of course it came back positive. "What drugs did it show?"

"We have to run more tests to identify the specific drugs. In the meantime, we've pumped his stomach, but unfortunately, depending on when he ingested the drugs, it may not be helpful."

"Is he okay?"

"He's alive. Still unresponsive. But his organs are working, and once we find out what specific drugs are in his system, we'll be able to treat him better."

"Why didn't you test for specific drugs?"

"Standard procedures are to do general toxicology first. Do you have any idea what he may have ingested?"

"No, I wasn't with him. I found him this morning."

"Was anyone else with him?"

"Yes. Two women were with him last night, but they left before I called the ambulance."

"Do you have any way of getting in touch with those women?"

If only... "I'm afraid I don't. I only know their first names."

"I see." She frowns. "But it's your opinion that Mr. Locke would not have ingested anything of his own accord?"

"I've known him a long time, Doctor. He's been sober for the last several years. He uses marijuana sometimes, takes a drink sometimes, but he stays away from the hard stuff."

"I see," she says again. "So he wouldn't have had anything illegal in his possession?"

"No. We're from the United States. I doubt it would've gotten past customs without a physician's note."

"That's true. All right, thank you."

"Wait. May I see him?"

Dr. Nelson pauses and presses her lips together. "He's not awake, but I suppose you can see him."

"Thank you."

"Follow me."

She leads me through the double doors into the emergency area. It's divided into separate bays, all equipped with curtains for privacy. The doctor pulls back the green curtain to the third bay, and I follow her in.

Dragon is lying on the bed, dressed in a blue hospital gown and covered with a thin white blanket. An oxygen mask sits on his nose, and an IV is inserted in his left hand. He's hooked up to various monitors that beep consistently. His face is pale, and his eyes are closed.

Looking at him is difficult, so I shift my gaze around. The treatment area is stocked with medical supplies, of course, including dressings, bandages, and syringes. A gallon-sized bottle of hand sanitizer sits on the counter. Absently, I squeeze some into my palms and slather it over my hands and arms.

Finally, I force myself to look back at Dragon. His skin may be pale, but at least it's not blue.

His heart monitor beeps, and his pulse ox is reading at about ninety-two. That's a little low, but the nurse assures me he's doing fine. Once she leaves, I sit in the chair next to Dragon's bed. Should I take his hand? The idea seems weird, so I don't.

I lean down close to his ear. "I need you to wake up, Dragon. We need you. The band needs you."

No response, of course. Not that I was expecting one.

A nurse comes in. "I can give you a call if anything changes. Are there any family members we should contact in the States?"

"He doesn't have any family," I say, still looking at Dragon's pale face. "I'm his family."

That's not true. Dragon does have family, but he doesn't have any relationship with them, and I wouldn't know how to contact them anyway.

"Good enough." The nurse touches my shoulder lightly. "He's going to be fine."

"When will he be released?"

"Not until he wakes up, and we don't expect that until later this afternoon. Then the doctors will probably want to keep him overnight for observation."

"Damn," I can't help saying.

"What's wrong?"

"He's a member of a rock band. We have a concert tonight. We're opening for Emerald Phoenix."

The nurse's jaw drops. "I'm going to that concert tonight. My friend went last night. She said the opening band was fantastic."

I look down at the tile floor. Normally a compliment like that would have me head over heels with excitement, but right now, all I can think about is Dragon. Dragon...and the fact that we may have just blown a big chance because of Jenny and Andrea.

"Thank you. I'm glad your friend enjoyed our music." I reach out and touch Dragon's shoulder lightly. "We had a wonderful time. But without Dragon, I don't see how we can go on tonight."

"I'll do everything I can, but I doubt the doctor will allow him to go until tomorrow."

"Yeah. I understand. I want what's best for him. That's the most important thing."

"I'm glad you see it that way. You're a good friend."

Am I, though?

If I were a good friend, I would've stayed with Dragon last night instead of becoming distracted by Brianna. I should have taken Dragon aside and tried to talk him out of the four-way he planned for us.

I look around the bay once more, taking in all the equipment, the supplies, the machines with their constant rhythmic beeping.

Beep...

Beep...

Beep...

The sound propels my anxiety, and I find myself holding my breath between beeps, as if that will somehow help Dragon. But it won't. I'm completely helpless in this situation.

I jerk when my phone dings with a text, and I welcome the respite from the monotony of the beeping.

It's Rory.

Jesse, can you come back to the hotel?
Jett says he needs to talk to you and me
together.

My heart sinks.

Sure enough, we've blown it.

CHAPTER FOUR

B r i a n n a

If only...

I know better than to play the *if only* game, but I can't help myself at the moment.

I look at Maddie. Her pretty lips are turned down into a frown. She's worried for her sister and brother, for their big chance.

I look at my brother Donny and his fiancée, Callie.

Callie has the same look on her face as Maddie. She's concerned, and rightly so. Jesse and Rory may have lost their shot for the band to make it big.

And I can think of so many *if onlys*...

If only I hadn't come here...

But I did.

If only I hadn't gone to bed with Jesse that first night...

But I did.

If only I hadn't talked Maddie into coming for the duration of the tour and putting off her last semester of college...

But I did.

If only I hadn't agreed to come back to the hotel last night with Maddie and Zane...

But I did.

And if only...

If only I hadn't gone with Jesse last night to his room...

But I did.

It was wonderful, and I can't bring myself to regret the act itself. But I have so much regret anyway. Regret that I even started this thing in the first place.

Why didn't I leave well enough alone?

How selfish was it to force myself along on this tour and become a distraction Jesse didn't need?

I should leave.

I want so desperately to fix this for Jesse, but I can't. I have no resources in the UK. I have no musical resources in the US, for that matter. My only idea was Brock, and he torched that in a millisecond.

But Brock was right. This is the big chance for the band, and they can't make do with an amateur drummer who hasn't played in ten years.

If only...

If only...

If only...

I want to go home.

To go home to the ranch, where I'm appreciated. Where I'm needed. Where I'm not anyone's distraction.

Dad would love it if I came running home. He'd put me to work right away, and I could dive into something—focus on something I love. That I've been groomed for my whole life.

My trees. My beautiful apple trees and peach trees.

And the Granny Smith orchard. Dad's going to expand it. Expand my favorite apple.

I had an idea in my head, one I meant to talk to Dad about when I finished college. I want to curate some artisanal goods from our orchards. With Aunt Marjorie's help, I could put together jams and jellies and butters.

If I hadn't forced myself along on this trip, he and I could be talking about those ideas now. It's only January, and there would have been enough time to look into sourcing and manufacturing, perhaps even getting an initial amount of product out by the fall.

But I didn't mention it to Dad...

I didn't mention it to him because it was more important that I come on this tour. That I be with Jesse Pike.

I put my childhood crush ahead of my family.

And I put it ahead of Jesse and the band.

How easy it would be to tell everyone I was flying home. That I changed my mind.

But then I look at Maddie...

Maddie, who I convinced to come—who I convinced to put off her last semester of college so she could stay for the entire tour.

Maddie, who always felt left out of the awesome foursome. Maddie, who always felt overshadowed by three amazing older siblings.

She's depending on me.

As much as I want to get the hell out of here, I cannot let her down.

Then I realize...

If the band can't fulfill their contract—if Emerald Phoenix considers them in breach—we will probably all be going home anyway.

I want to cry. I want to cry and cry and cry, let the tears flow freely until my whole body is racked with sobs.

But I also want to put my fist through a wall.

I want to punch right through the drywall and make my knuckles bleed.

Because...

If I hadn't been so selfish... If I hadn't left Dad—who's only now recovered enough from his gunshot wound to work outside in the orchards we both love— and forced my way onto this trip...

Perhaps none of this would be happening now.

Callie rises. "We're going to head up."

Donny scribbles his signature on the check and stands as well. "Are you two okay?"

Maddie swallows and nods. "As okay as I guess we can be. Me at least."

I'm not sure how to answer my brother's question. I'm a lot of things right now, but none of them are okay.

I simply nod.

No one wants to hear me talk about how this is all my fault.

No one wants to hear me say what a selfish and horny bitch I was about this whole thing.

None of them know why I did it.

None of them know what's happened between Jesse and me.

Because if they did?

They'd blame me, just as I'm blaming myself.

Only Maddie and I sit at the table, and neither of us has touched our breakfast.

My eggs are cold and clammy, and the streaky bacon is congealed with fat. My awful coffee remains untouched other than a few sips.

"I don't know what to do," Maddie says.

"I don't either, Mads."

She scratches the side of her head. "Do you think the two

of us should..."

"Should what?"

She sighs and looks down at the table, at her own plate that has hardly been touched. "Maybe we should just go home, Bree. I can go back to school. There's still time. The new semester hasn't even started yet. Right now, I'm just another thing for Jesse and Rory to worry about."

Well...she brought it up.

"Are you sure, Maddie?"

She frowns. "Not really. I'm not sure of anything right now. Maybe I should ask Rory and Jesse."

And as if Maddie's voice conjured him out of thin air, Jesse walks into the restaurant. His gaze locks with mine.

"There he is," I say to Maddie.

"Jesse!" She waves at him.

He shakes his head, walks by us and out of the restaurant. And most likely...out of my life.

CHAPTER FIVE

Jesse

I don't like ignoring my sister the way I just did, but I can't be distracted by her or Brianna Steel right now. Brock and Rory—along with Jett Draconis—are waiting for me in Jett's suite. I had to walk through the breakfast area to get to the elevators.

Well, I didn't have to. It was a shortcut. Had I known my sister and Brianna were still sitting in there, I would have taken the long way around.

But I'm in a hurry.

I can't keep Jett waiting. We've already screwed up enough.

I take the elevator to the top floor of the hotel and walk to Jett's suite.

I draw a breath and knock.

Jett himself opens the door.

"Hey, Jesse."

I open my mouth, but then I don't know what to say. Do I apologize profusely for screwing this whole thing up? I mean, it wasn't me. It was Dragon, though most likely through no fault of his own.

Unless you count the fact that he went to bed with two women when he had no clue who they were. Then yes, it *was* his fault.

Jett's wife, Heather, along with Brock and Rory, are sitting in the living area. Their suite makes Brock and Rory's look like a slum, but that's the last time I consider the immense size.

"Hey, Jess," Rory says.

"Come on in," Jett says. He gestures to the living area. "Have a seat."

I take an unoccupied chair. Heather sits on a love seat, and Rory and Brock sit side by side on the sofa, holding hands.

"How's Dragon?" Brock asks.

"He should recover. We don't know yet what he ingested, but his toxicology was positive."

"How do they know it was positive if they don't know what he ingested?" Brock asks.

"I don't know, man." I rub my hand over my hair, rise, pace a few steps. "It's the way they do it over here or something. Or the way they do it everywhere, for all I know."

"Brock..." From Rory.

"It's okay," I say. "I wish I had more information. All I know is they pumped his stomach, and according to his doctor, he will recover. He was still asleep when I left. I haven't been able to talk to him."

"When will he be released?" Jett asks.

I sit back down. "They expect him to wake up later today. But he probably won't be released until tomorrow."

Rory bites her lip.

"I'm so sorry," I say to Jett. "He's been clean for so long. If it's any consolation, I don't think he took anything. I think he was drugged by the two women he was with."

"That's been known to happen," Jett says.

The look on his face is unreadable. Is he being understanding? Or is he just mad as a hornet? I'm guessing the latter.

"So," Jett says, taking Heather's hand. "I owe you an apology, Jesse."

My mouth drops open.

I play his words over in my head, wondering if I got them right. I'm exhausted, freaked out, worried for Dragon, worried for the band.

Did he just say he owes *me* an apology?

"Pick your jaw up off the floor, Jess," Rory says.

I close my mouth and swallow. "I'm sorry. I think the only one who owes anyone an apology around here is me."

"Why?" Jett asks. "Did you force your drummer to take drugs?"

I shake my head. "What... I don't understand..."

"Zane came to me early this morning. He told me what happened between him and your sister and her friend last night."

Right. Zane. Maddie and Brianna. All the anger I was feeling last night—all the anger I channeled into fucking Brianna when I should've been with Dragon, talking him out of bedding two randos.

"Zane feels terrible about what happened. He says he didn't know Maddie was your sister."

I still have no words. I probably look like a moron sitting here with my mouth half open.

"I won't lie to you," Jett says. "Zane can be a player. He has a weakness for groupies—not that those two are groupies. He also has a weakness for beautiful young women. I'm glad nothing happened."

"Yeah." I finally speak. "Me too."

"I'm sure that put a bad taste in your mouth about the

band."

"Why?" I say, echoing his own sentiment. "Did you make him do it?"

"Of course not!"

Does he think I was serious? Man, I'm screwing this up big time. If they weren't thinking about sending Dragonlock packing, they probably are now.

"I didn't mean—"

"I know you didn't." Jett gives me a smile as he nods. "I think we're all a little on edge at the moment. Ease up. We're going to work this out."

I raise my eyebrows. "We are? How?"

"Jesse," Rory says. "Jett may have a solution to our problem."

My eyebrows rise farther. Why the hell would he want to help us? Surely not because he feels bad about Zane going after my sister and Brianna.

"Oh?" is all I say.

"I know I'm not Zane's keeper," Jett says, "any more than you're Dragon's keeper. But you're the leader of your band, as I am, and you, like I do, probably feel a sense of responsibility to the whole group. You're feeling like you're at fault."

So he gets it. He really gets it. "Man, I sure as hell do."

"I have to tell myself the same thing about the band. But they're all grown-ups, and I can't control Zane's actions any more than you can control Dragon's."

"I'm sorry." I shake my head. "What exactly are you getting at?"

Jett smiles. "We travel with a large staff, as you probably already know. That includes extra musicians who can pick up the slack if something happens. In other words, we have a drummer for you."

"But you... Our contract..."

"Yeah, your contract. All five of you signed, and Dragon is unable to perform. But rather than make a huge issue of that, why not find a solution? And I think we have one."

"But your drummer... I'm sure he's great, but he doesn't know any of our stuff."

"Derek's not the backup we normally travel with," Jett says. "Our backup was unavailable, but Derek is amazing on percussions. He'll pick it up. You can rehearse this afternoon. You know I wouldn't be traveling with subpar musicians."

"No, of course not."

"Jesse," Rory says, "this fixes our problem." She looks at Jett. "I can't thank you enough."

Yes, I should be thanking him.

"Yeah, of course, man. Thank you. You don't have to do this."

"That's where you're wrong," he says. "All our contracts with all the venues specify an opener, so if we don't have an opener, we're in breach of contract. This fixes it for all of us. And Dragon will probably be back to work soon. But if he can't do the rest of the UK tour, he'll join us when we get to Paris."

I'm still in shock. "I... I just never imagined..."

"Dude," Jett says, "don't you think I've been where you are? People helped me along the way, and I try to pay it forward when I can."

"You've already done that by inviting us on this tour with you."

"Yeah, and I want you and your sister up there singing your hearts out tonight. You two are fabulous together. You don't need a specific drummer to make that work."

"There's more good news," Brock says.

More good news? The words don't even make sense to me at this point. How can there be more good news?

"What's that?" I ask.

"I've been looking at the numbers from the concert last night. With regard to merchandise, we've almost broken even."

"That's great for the first night."

"No," Brock says. "You're not understanding me. After just one night—one concert—you sold enough merch to pay me back for my entire investment. All that's left is my two percent, and that won't be calculated until the end of the tour. But other than the two percent, it's all profit from here on out, dude."

Again my jaw drops. And not because Brock called me "dude."

How can this all be happening?

How can all these people be on my side?

Seems I've had to work my ass off for every little thing I've gotten, and once our big break came, I thought it was ruined.

I thought it was ruined because that's how Jesse Pike's life goes. Jesse Pike is not Brock Steel. Or Donny Steel. Things don't go Jesse Pike's way all the time.

But it's not the end.

Things are still going our way, despite the fact that I got distracted last night with Brianna.

I can't take that chance again.

No more distractions.

"We're thinking," Rory says, "that it might be better for Dragon to stay here. Recuperate fully. And then join us in Paris. We can use Jett's drummer until then."

"I can't leave Dragon here alone," I say.

Rory reaches toward me and places her hand on my arm.

"He needs a few days to heal, Jess. To detox from the drugs."

"I... I don't know. I have to talk to his doctors. To him."

"There's no time to get back to the hospital today," Rory says. "We've got to meet the new drummer and practice. We're running out of time."

My sister's right, of course. But someone has to be there when Dragon wakes up.

Somebody who doesn't have anything else to do.

Maddie.

Maddie and Brianna.

CHAPTER SIX

Brianna

"I feel so useless," Maddie says to me.

The two of us are back in our room, and we're not sure what to do with ourselves.

We saw the big sites on the guided tour, and we spent some time in museums and strolling the streets of London by ourselves. We didn't get our meat pie on Fleet Street, but I couldn't eat now.

We haven't done much shopping either. Not that I'm a huge shopper, and neither is Maddie. Maybe she would be if she had more money.

None of it really matters. The last time I went shopping with a purpose was to buy the dragon belt buckle for Jesse for Christmas. So yeah, I'm not feeling the urge to shop.

Maddie's phone buzzes, and her eyebrows rise. "It's Jesse. He wants to talk to the two of us. He and Rory both."

My heart races just at Jesse's name.

But I draw in a deep breath, try to relax it back into a normal rhythm. Jesse's not mine. I can't let him be distracted by me anymore.

"Okay," I say, willing my voice not to shake.

"Oh my God." Maddie beams. "They want us to go to Jett Draconis's suite."

I say nothing. I have no words.

Maddie taps on her phone. "I'm telling them we'll be right there. Do you know where Donny and Callie are?"

"I don't. Probably in their room."

"All right. We didn't make any plans with them today anyway. Let's just go to Jett's suite, I guess."

I take a quick look in the mirror. It doesn't really matter what I look like. Jesse and I are over. I'll never be able to forgive myself for taking him away from Dragon last night.

I look fine. My hair is in a ponytail, and I'm wearing regular old jeans, a hoodie, and my walking sneakers. I don't have any makeup on except for a little bit of lip tint.

And again...

It doesn't matter.

I follow Maddie through the eating area to the elevators, and we ascend to the top floor where Jett's suite is.

Maddie knocks on the door, and I stand slightly behind her.

I feel like a shadow this morning. Like a part of me is missing. I'll just have to learn to live without it.

To my surprise, Brock opens the door. "Hey, Bree, Maddie. Come on in."

Jett Draconis is there with his wife, Heather. Rory sits on the couch, and Jesse—gorgeous Jesse—is sitting in a chair. He looks over his shoulder, his gaze meeting mine.

Then he looks away.

But in that split second, I saw the guilt in his sunken dark eyes, the regret and the consternation.

"You two know everyone here, don't you?" Brock asks.

"Yeah, of course," Maddie says. "Jett, Heather, it's nice to see you again."

"Good to see you two," Jett says. "I want to apologize to both of you for Zane's behavior last night."

I stare at Jett. God...this means everyone in the room knows what Maddie and I almost did. I look to the floor, hoping a giant hole will appear and swallow me up. I say nothing, and to my surprise, Maddie speaks.

"I should be apologizing," she says. "Brianna and I really shouldn't have been—"

"No, you shouldn't have," Jesse cuts her off. "But we're all adults here, even though it's hard for me to remember that sometimes."

Maddie apologized? I didn't see that coming. She was so angry with me, and—

"We need a favor from you two," Jesse continues. "Rory and I, and the band."

"Of course," Maddie says. "What do you need?"

I still haven't said anything. This conversation is surreal. No one has spoken directly to me, and what would I say anyway?

Jesse clears his throat. "Someone needs to be at the hospital for Dragon. For when he wakes up. I've already called and told the staff that the two of you would be coming over to act in my stead."

News to me. The last thing I want to do is babysit Dragon Locke.

But if this is what Jesse needs from me, I'll do it.

Maddie gazes to the floor, looking crestfallen. "Well, yeah, sure, Jess. Whatever you need."

"It would be best for me to be there," Jesse says, "but Jett has arranged for a drummer for us until Dragon's back on his feet, which means we need to get him up to speed on our numbers this afternoon. Dragon will probably wake up sometime before this evening, and I don't want him to be alone when he does."

"Yeah, of course. Sure," Maddie says again.

I simply nod.

Not exactly how I expected to spend the afternoon, but because Jesse asked, I will do it. I will do whatever he needs me to do.

Which probably includes staying the hell away from him.

"I've arranged for our limo to take you to the hospital," Jett says.

"They can take a cab," Jesse says.

"Don't be silly. All the band members are here at the hotel right now, and our driver isn't doing anything. It won't be a problem at all."

"But they may be at the hospital for a while," Jesse says.

"Whatever you need, Jesse," Maddie says once more. "If you need me to help watch over Dragon, I'll do it."

"I will too," I finally say. "With two of us there, someone can be with him at all times."

Jesse looks at me for the first time. His brown eyes are even more sad and sunken.

"Thank you." He stares deeply into my eyes. "Thank you so much."

The sincerity in his tone is more than clear. He's grateful and earnest, and I won't let him down. I've done enough to let him down already.

Jett rises. "The driver is waiting for you. Do you two need to go to your room and get anything?"

"I just need to grab my purse," I say.

"Yeah, me too." Maddie walks to Jesse, pulls him out of

his chair, and embraces him. "I'm so sorry, Jesse."

Jesse kisses the top of her head. "It's okay, sis. Everything's going to work out fine."

But from the look on his face, I don't think Jesse is convinced.

All I can do is what he asks.

Go with Maddie to the hospital, watch over Dragon.

Maddie lets go of Jesse, and again he gazes at me.

I want to launch myself into his arms, bury my head in his hard chest. Tell him how sorry I am about everything. That I'll take care of Dragon. That I'll do anything. That I'll let him go if that's what he needs.

But I don't.

Instead, I follow Maddie out the door. We take the elevator to our room, and we both grab our purses.

Then, without speaking, we head back down, walk through the lobby, and find a large limo parked right outside the entrance to the hotel. A driver, dressed all in black, waits for us.

"Are you Ms. Pike and Ms. Steel?" he asks.

"Yes," Maddie says.

"I'm Adolpho. I'm here to take you to the hospital." Adolpho holds the door to the back seat.

Maddie climbs in, and I climb in next to her.

Adolpho takes his place in the front seat, and we're off.

Off to spend the day at the hospital, waiting for Dragon to wake up.

CHAPTER SEVEN

Jesse

Derek Bell, the drummer that Emerald Phoenix so graciously loaned to us, is a huge talent. He may not have Dragon's intuition, but what he lacks in instinct he makes up for in pure finesse. He's a nearly perfect percussionist with regard to technique.

He didn't miss a beat during our first rehearsal.

I'm so damned grateful that I didn't mention the fact that both Jake and Cage were a little late coming in on the first run-through.

I'm content with Derek's skills after rehearsing each number once.

We need to save our energy for tonight's concert.

"Thanks, man," I say, shaking his hand. "I don't know what we'd do without you."

"Not a problem. Sorry about your guy. So he's an addict, huh?" Derek shakes his head. "I've never met an addict who didn't relapse."

Something bites the back of my neck, but I breathe through it. Best not to piss off the guy who's saving our ass. "Dragon's not like that. He's been sober for years."

"Doesn't matter. I've been in this business a long time. It's best to stay away from addicts. They always let you down."

Oh. My. God.

Does he not realize that Dragon is a friend of mine? He picked the wrong person to say this—

Rory slides between us, holding out her hand to Derek. "We can't thank you enough for stepping in."

Derek skates his gaze over Rory in a way that makes my skin crawl. Good thing she's got that massive pink ring on her left hand.

"Anything for you, pretty lady." Derek smiles at Rory.

"Yeah, you have our gratitude." I yank Rory away from Derek and out of earshot. "I officially hate him."

"Don't be ridiculous, Jess. He's saving our ass."

"He said some shitty things about Dragon. About addicts in general. And I didn't like the way he was looking at you."

"You're just being a big brother," she says. "He was perfectly respectful, and he couldn't say enough about you and me singing together."

"I didn't hear any of that."

"Maybe he just said it to me."

"Yeah. I'll bet he did."

"Knock all this off, Jess. Christ."

She's right. I'll put up with Derek and his snide comments about Dragon. I'll even put up with him looking like he'd like to have Rory for lunch.

I don't have a choice.

Besides, we have other things to figure out.

"I know you and Brock took care of the contractual issues," I say to her. "How much is it going to cost us? To have Derek play?"

"That's the beauty of it, Jess," she says. "Jett and Heather feel so badly about what happened to Dragon that they're covering the performance hours for Derek for the remainder of the UK portion of the tour."

I shake my head. "That's not right, Rory."

"You're so much like Mom and Dad." She squeezes my shoulder. "Sometimes it's okay to take a gift when it's offered. We worked hard for this, Jesse. And we don't deserve to have our lives screwed over because Dragon couldn't stay away from two groupies."

She's right, of course.

"And this isn't your fault," she continues, reading my mind. "We all thought Dragon had a hold on his addiction."

I narrow my gaze. "He *did,* Ror. He had to have been drugged."

"We won't know that for sure until he wakes up...which should be happening any time now."

I grab my phone out of my pocket to check the time. "I should get over to the hospital. He's going to want to talk to me."

"Jesse, no." She grips my shoulders. "You need to stay here. You need to meditate or do whatever you do before a concert. Maddie and Brianna are there. They can take care of him."

"You don't understand." I shake my head. "I know things about Dragon that no one knows. And I—"

She shakes me, still holding my shoulders. Literally shakes me. Even though I'm close to twice her weight.

"Stop it. We're lucky we can go on tonight without Dragon. You need to be here. Focused. Dragon is fine. We know he's going to be okay. You can go see him tomorrow before we leave for Edinburgh."

Again, I know she's right. But I'm tense. So damned tense.

I could see if the spa could get me in for another massage.

No. Then I would be *too* relaxed to sing well.

A certain amount of tension is necessary before you perform—at least it is for me. It's that tension that keeps you on your toes, keeps you from screwing up when you're onstage.

"I know you're right," I say, "but Dragon and I have a connection that I don't have with the rest of you guys."

Rory tilts her head to the side, as if she's trying to figure out what I mean.

"I know that sounds weird, but it's just... He trusts me, Ror. He trusts me, and I can't let him down."

"But he's letting *us* down. Don't you see?"

"Not if it wasn't his fault."

"It may not be his fault that he got drugged, Jesse, but it was his fault that he took two women he didn't know to bed."

She's not wrong, and it could've easily been me as well. And then what would we have done? The drummer may be replaceable, but the lead singer is not.

No more groupies for me. Not ever.

Cage and I talked about screwing our way across Europe, but that won't be happening. Which means I won't be screwing at all, because I have to stay away from Brianna Steel.

She wants more than I can give her.

I heave out a sigh. "All right."

"You and I are going to have a little chat with Cage and Jake," Rory says. "And then we're going to get a light dinner sent up to Brock's and my suite. Okay?"

I nod and follow her to the elevator. When it arrives on her floor, we head to Rory's suite.

Cage and Jake are waiting outside the door.

"Where've you been?" Jake asks.

"You mean you knew to meet us here?"

Jake nods. "Yeah, Rory texted us."

"Apparently we're going to have a *Come to Jesus* talk with my sister," I say.

Rory hovers a key card over the reader, and the door opens. "Sorry. I thought Brock would be here to let you in."

"Apparently not," Cage says.

"Well, come on in. Take a seat."

"Yes, ma'am," Jake says.

"Cool it with that shit," Rory says, raising her eyebrows.

"Come on, cuz," Cage says. "We know what you're about to say. And the fact of the matter is we agree with you."

"Oh?"

"I'm not sure you know what she has to say," I say.

"Nope, Jake and I have been talking," Cage continues. "We're going to stay the hell away from the groupies. We don't need what happened to Dragon to happen to us."

"So you all believe he was drugged?" Rory says.

"Absolutely," Jake says, nodding. "He's been clean for so long."

"Except for the pot and the booze," Rory reminds him.

"Nope," Cage says. "Dragon could handle that. Right, Jess?"

"Yeah." I resist the urge to bite my lower lip. "At least that's what I thought. I want to suggest that you all stay away from all that at this point, though. At least during the rest of this tour."

"Agreed," Rory says. "All four of you need to keep your dicks inside your pants. Got it?"

"Okay, okay, Mom."

Rory narrows her gaze at Jake's words. "Call me whatever the hell you need to call me, Jake. Just keep the mouse in the house."

"Mouse?" Jake waggles his eyebrows.

"Quit that," I say. "You know she's taken, and she's my sister, for God's sake."

Jake raises his hands in mock surrender. "Simmer down, man. Fuck."

"Look, guys," I continue. "I know we all had this idea of groupies fawning all over us, of screwing our way around Europe. That plan is officially off-limits. This is serious. We all know what this means for the band and what this could mean for our careers. And even if it goes nowhere? We're still going to make more money on this tour than we've ever made in our lives. I don't know about you all, but Rory and I need that money."

"Rory is engaged to a Steel," Cage reminds us.

"Yeah? Well, she and I still need to give this money to our parents to help them rebuild their winery. So no more fucking around."

Brock enters then. "Dinner come yet?" He closes the door.

"Not yet," Rory says. "But the guys are all on board. Celibacy for the rest of the trip."

"Excuse me?" Brock says.

"Not us," Rory says. "But I don't need to worry about you drugging me."

Brock wraps his arm around Rory's waist. "Nope. Besides, I'd never want anything to dull your senses when we're together."

I put my hands over my ears. "For God's sake, you two. Get a damned room."

"We have a room, Jesse," Brock says. "You're in it."

"Then please don't make us listen to any more of this. I promised we'd all eat a light dinner together and then relax until we have to leave for the venue."

"And we will," Rory says. "The food should be here soon."

"Everything's going to work out fine," Brock says, grinning. "After all, I want you guys to be stars. You know... So I can get my two percent of your merch."

I roll my eyes. Brock needs our two percent like he needs a hole in the head, but I'm the one who insisted he take a cut since he fronted us the money. Which apparently has pretty much all been paid back after one night. Amazing.

A knock on the door then, and Brock rises. Two servers bring in two trolleys of food. Brock signs the bill, and then we take a look at what Rory ordered.

She wasn't kidding when she said light. Green salad, fruit salad, and broiled chicken fingers.

"Ror, we're going to need a little more than this."

She hands me a napkin. "There's plenty. You eat as much chicken as you can handle. If we go through it all, we'll order more. But you need your protein, and there's enough sugar in the fruit to keep you going. But there is no way I was going feed you red meat tonight, which is hard to digest, or anything with added sugar, which will make you crash."

Jake grabs a plate and fills it. "I hate it when your sister's right all the time."

"Yeah," I say dryly. "It's a drag." I rise to grab a plate, next in line after Jake, when my phone buzzes in my back pocket. My heart jumps. "It's Maddie," I say. "Dragon's awake."

CHAPTER EIGHT

Brianna

The most I know about Dragon Locke is that he and Jesse seem to be pretty close, and he spent time at my parents' last party talking to my sister, Diana.

Which in itself was strange.

Diana is an academic. A professional. An architect, currently interning with one of the best architecture firms in Denver.

She and Dragon have zilch in common.

He and Jesse have more in common, at least. They're both musicians. But Jesse is a vocalist and a guitarist, and Dragon is a percussionist.

Quite different, but Jesse thought enough of Dragon to bring him into his band and name it after him.

Although admittedly, Dragon Locke is a very cool name, and it makes a cool band name.

Maddie and I have been taking turns sitting in Dragon's room with him. He was moved from the accident and emergency department to a ward. Apparently his condition wasn't bad enough to merit a private room. Things are different here.

During my time off from sitting with him, I've walked around the hospital so many times that I now have the place memorized. In the cafeteria, I discovered digestive biscuits—

whole wheat cookies with a thin coating of chocolate. They're surprisingly good.

The fact that Emerald Phoenix loaned Dragonlock their backup drummer helps ease the load of guilt I'm carrying, but I still feel like Jesse will be blaming me for the fact that he wasn't with Dragon last night. He could barely look at me when we were in Jett's suite.

I walk back to the room, and Maddie shrieks. "Thank God you're back, Bree. I think he's waking up."

Sure enough, Dragon's eyelids are fluttering.

What's he going to think when he sees the two of us? And not Jesse?

"Dragon," Maddie says. "It's me. Maddie. Jesse's sister."

He turns toward the sound of Maddie's voice. "Jess?" he croaks out.

"Jesse's back at the hotel. Brianna and I are here. You know. Brianna Steel."

"What... Where..."

"You're in the hospital, Dragon." Maddie opens her mouth to keep talking but then closes it.

Yeah, probably best not to spout out all the details until he's a little more conscious.

"How are you feeling?" I ask.

What a dumb question. He's probably feeling like crap.

"I don't..."

"It's okay," Maddie says. "You don't have to talk. But good news, the concert—"

He jerks upward in bed and then winces in pain.

"Dragon—" Maddie says.

"Concert. I've got to get to the concert."

"No, you can't." Maddie tries to calm him. "They got a

backup drummer. Everything's fine. The concert is going on. All you need to do is get better."

"I don't understand. What happened?" He falls back down on the bed.

"Relax. Everything's going to be fine." I walk out of the ward and find a nurse. "Excuse me. Mr. Locke has woken up."

She nods. "Someone will be in right away."

I return, and Maddie is patting Dragon's hand. "I promise. It's okay. Jesse would be here if he could, but he has to prepare for the concert."

Dragon's eyes are closed again.

"Did he fall back asleep?" I ask.

"I don't think so." Maddie tilts her head. "Maybe he did. It's probably best for him."

"All right, what do we have here?" A nurse walks toward us, picks up Dragon's chart.

"He woke up for a few minutes," I say.

"Yeah, he was kind of agitated," Maddie says.

The nurse touches his shoulder. "Mr. Locke? Are you awake?"

His eyes slide open. "What happened?"

"You ingested a large amount of fentanyl last night," she says. "You're lucky to be alive, Mr. Locke."

His eyes widen. "I didn't... I would never..."

"It's okay, Dragon," Maddie says. "We think you were probably drugged by those two women."

"What two women?"

The nurse grabs a pen and flips through some papers on a clipboard. "What's the last thing you remember, Mr. Locke?"

Dragon closes his eyes and winces. "Oh yeah. Two women. We got into the limo. But there were four of them, and Jesse..."

Jesse? My neck prickles.

"I don't remember getting back to the hotel."

"Retroactive amnesia," the nurse says. "It's common in instances like this. His toxicology results show fentanyl and Rohypnol."

"You mean roofies?" I ask. "The date rape drug?"

"Yes. Rohypnol, which is probably what's causing the retroactive amnesia. But if that were the only thing he ingested, he would've been just fine. It was the fentanyl he overdosed on."

"Someone fucking drugged me?" Dragon asks, his voice no more than a whisper.

"If you're sure you didn't ingest it yourself, then yes, someone drugged you. But Mr. Locke, if you have no memory of the time, you could've ingested it yourself."

"What does it matter?" Maddie asks. "One way or another, he's going to be okay."

The nurse smiles. "Yes. He's going to be okay. But the person who filled out your paperwork last night—a Mr. Jesse Pike—indicated that you *are* an addict."

Dragon closes his eyes. "Yes," he says softly.

"So you will be detoxing. The next few days will be hard on you. You can either stay here in the hospital, or you can go home."

"Home? You mean back to the US?"

The nurse shakes her head. "We don't really recommend you traveling for the next few days. We can give you some methadone, which may ease your detox symptoms. And then, of course, you know the drill. You stay away from the stuff."

Dragon raises his hand to his head, trembling. "But I have to be... The band..."

"The band is going to be fine," Maddie says. "I've talked to Jesse and Rory."

"Man, they're going to be so pissed at me," Dragon says.

"Jesse doesn't believe you took anything. He thinks the two women you were with drugged you."

Dragon blinks. Blinks again. "Two women? Two women, and I don't remember? What the hell?"

Okay, weird. A moment ago, he remembered the four women and getting into the limo. His mind is still a mess.

The nurse smiles. "Mr. Locke, try to be happy that you're alive."

He nods.

"I'll be back to check on you in a bit. Are you feeling hungry at all?"

"No. I kind of feel like shit."

"You may be experiencing some symptoms of withdrawal already. I'll get the doctor to order some methadone."

"I know what to expect," he says. "I've detoxed before."

"Then you know it's not pretty," the nurse says.

"Lady, none of my life has been pretty." Dragon frowns, almost scowling. "Detox is the least of it. And I don't want any methadone."

"That's your call." She leaves quickly.

Dragon's words make my heart ache. Nobody really knows anything about Dragon Locke. Except for Jesse.

"I'm texting Jesse," Maddie says. "He wants to know when you're awake."

"Man," Dragon says. "He's going to hate me."

"My brother could never hate you," Maddie says. "He's the most loving person I know."

I resist raising my eyebrows. Jesse is the most loving

person Maddie knows? First I've heard of that.

"You ladies should go to the concert," Dragon says.

Maddie bites her lip.

"No," I say. "Jesse asked me to make sure you're okay, so I'm not leaving your side."

Maddie drops her jaw and looks at me. "Bree?"

"Someone has to stay with him, Mads. You go to the concert. Go with Brock, Donny, and Callie. I'm not leaving."

"You should get some dinner."

I point to the package of McVitie's—the digestive cookies—that I bought at the little market in the hospital. "I'm good."

"Oh, come on, Bree."

"Mads, let me do this. Jesse and Rory are your brother and sister. You're the one who deserves to be at that concert. I want to stay here."

"Brianna, I know you're a big fan of the band."

"So I'll see the next concert. It will be fine. You get ready to go."

She finishes texting Jesse. "If you're sure..."

"Yeah, just call a cab."

"Don't have to. Adolpho gave me his card, remember?"

"He'll probably be busy transporting the band to the venue," I say. "Call a cab. Go back to the hotel and change clothes. Text Donny and Callie and go to the concert with them. Please, Maddie."

She finally consents, and I let out a breath.

I want her to go. I promised her a good time on this trip.

And now I have to pay the penance for my own sins. For being so manipulative. For keeping Jesse distracted when he should've been paying attention to the band.

This is my punishment, and I'll take it gladly.

CHAPTER NINE

Jesse

With everything in me, I want to go to Dragon.

"You can't," Rory says, again reading my mind.

Of all my siblings, I'm closest to Rory. She would probably say she's closest to Callie because they're only two years apart. But Rory and I share something that Callie doesn't—our love and passion for music. Especially since Rory joined the band. It's like we can finish each other's sentences and read each other's minds. It's damned annoying most of the time.

Despite the fact that Dragon tried to take her to bed not so long ago, I still feel like I should be there for him. I still feel like I let him down.

"Maddie and Brianna are there," Rory continues.

"Maddie and Brianna don't know Dragon. He barely knows them. I'm not sure he knows Brianna at all."

"Are you kidding me?" Rory says. "Brianna and the rest of the awesome foursome have been following you guys around at Murphy's for the last year, ever since they came of age and could get in."

"Yeah, but Dragon never pays attention to them. He knows Maddie because she's our sister, but Brianna?"

"Think about what you're saying, Jesse. Of course he knows Brianna. She's beautiful."

My sister's not wrong.

Brianna Steel's image haunts me.

"I know that look," Rory says. "You're blaming yourself again. Don't. Think of the big picture. The band. This chance that we have. Don't you go running over to that hospital, Jesse. There isn't time before the concert."

My sister's wrong. I *should* be blaming myself, but instead I was thinking about Brianna, about how my lips feel against hers, how my cock feels inside her. I wipe the picture from my mind.

"I know."

Cage and Jake excused themselves after finishing dinner, so it's just Rory, Brock, and me now.

"Do I need to put you on a leash?" my sister asks.

"For God's sake, Ror."

She narrows her eyes. "I see it on your face, Jess. Your instinct is to go over to that hospital. You think you can get there. A quick ride there and back, just to check. But we're leaving for the venue in an hour. An *hour*, Jess. There isn't time."

"I could go to the venue from the hospital," I say.

"No," she says adamantly, sounding strikingly like our mother.

And she's right, of course.

I must stay.

I must stay with the band. The band has to be my priority. Not Dragon. Not Brianna.

But the band.

I draw in a breath. "Do you trust me enough to go back to my room and try to focus for a bit?"

"Of course I do." She kisses my cheek. "Now go. I will see

you down at the entrance in forty-seven minutes exactly."

I nod, leave Brock and Rory's suite, and head to my own room, which is only one door down.

When Rory got the room for me, after I was suffering terrible jet lag when we first got here, she was bound and determined to make sure she could keep an eye on me. Hence the room next to hers. And I was happy to have it.

Very happy to have it last night, when I fucked Brianna Steel.

Still, I should've stayed in the room with Dragon. My original room. And all of this could've been avoided—

No! I cannot keep going there.

I must keep my mind on the band.

I lie down on my bed, visualize. Go through our entire concert in my head.

I don't have to worry about nodding off. Not when the adrenaline is already starting to flow.

I visualize the entire concert, visualize the audience's thundering applause, visualize...

Brianna Steel.

In the front row.

Standing, like she did last night, her tits filling out that Dragonlock tee.

I jerk upward. "Stop it," I say aloud.

Then I head to the bathroom, check myself in the mirror, change into my outfit for the concert.

Black jeans. Black shirt. Black boots.

Simple, but it works.

Rory of course will wear something sexy. I hate seeing her dress like that, but even *I* know it works for the band. My sister is considered the most beautiful woman in our small town. She may as well use it to the band's advantage.

At least I don't have to worry about male groupies trying to get in her pants. Brock won't let anyone near her.

I laugh out loud. I never thought I'd be thankful for a Steel, but I'm grateful that Rory is very much taken.

I make sure I have my phone and wallet. Everything else we need is already at the venue. It will be packed up tonight because tomorrow we move to Edinburgh.

I take the elevator down to the first floor, and when the doors open, I see Maddie standing before me.

I drop my jaw. "What are you doing here?"

"Don't worry. Brianna is with Dragon. She insisted I come to the concert tonight, Jesse."

"She did?"

"Yeah. For some strange reason, she really wants to look after Dragon. And you and Rory are my siblings, not hers. I want to see the concert, Jess."

"We're leaving now."

"Well, yeah, you and the band are leaving. I can take a cab to the venue. I want to change."

I nod. This trip isn't just about Rory, the band, or me. It's about Maddie too. It's about giving our little sister something to remember. She put off her last semester of college for this, and if what she wants is to see our band perform at every concert, that's what she'll have.

"I'm sorry," I say.

"For what?"

"For making you sit with Dragon all day."

She grabs my hand and squeezes it. "Jesse, I was glad to do it. And Brianna's still there. You don't have anything to worry about. Dragon's going to be fine."

I nod, give her a quick hug, and then watch as she gets into the elevator.

I head to the entrance, where the rest of the band stands. The limo is waiting.

"Thank God," Rory says.

"You didn't really think..."

"No, Jesse. I trust you. But there's something between you and Dragon that the rest of us don't understand. That's okay." She gives me a quick hug. "I know this is killing you. But you need to be in top form tonight, Jess. We need to show all of Emerald Phoenix that they were not wrong to put their faith in us."

Yeah. Doesn't seem to be bothering Rory nearly as much that Zane Michaels tried to get our littlest sister in bed last night.

But Jett was mortified, so I know Zane will be keeping his hands to himself for the rest of the tour.

★ ★ ★

The concert goes great again, and we're well received, getting another standing ovation from the crowd who came to see Emerald Phoenix.

Rory and I were totally in sync, despite my worries about Dragon. Though I thought I could hear what was lacking in Derek's percussion performance—Dragon's unique artistry—I have to admit that he was technical perfection. He came in on time and never missed a beat on every number.

No encore of course, so as soon as we're gone, I head straight to Derek, holding out my hand. He did an amazing job, so I'm letting the things he said about Dragon and the way he looked at Rory go. Trying to, anyway.

"Thanks so much, man. You were terrific."

Derek wipes perspiration off his forehead and then slicks his dark-blond hair back. "Glad to do it. I love to play, but I don't get to very often. I'm usually on hand as backup to the backup. This was a coup, since Emerald Phoenix's normal backup couldn't make it, but I doubted I'd get to play. Man, when I heard you guys rock this place last night, I was impressed."

"Thanks." I'm not sure what else I should say. The guy's a great drummer, and he got us out of a jam, but something about him rubs me the wrong way. Maybe I'm just still pissed about his comments about Dragon and addicts in general.

"You guys are going places," Derek says. "You and your sister have something I'm not sure I've ever seen or heard. Part of it is that you come from the same genes, so your voices are slightly similar in the way they mix. But it's also your chemistry onstage. It's more than brother-and-sister chemistry, but obviously not lovers' chemistry either."

"I should hope not," I say, wondering what's up with this guy. He seems to say things without thinking.

"Yeah, I knew that wasn't right now that I'm thinking about it." He strokes his chin. "But it's unique, man. I'm not sure I've heard anything like it, not since... Man, I'm not that old, but I have to go back to Sonny and Cher. They still had it even after they divorced."

There he goes again, saying something without thinking about all the meaning. "Cher is awesome," I say, "but I hope you're not comparing me to Sonny."

"No, man. Not at all. I'm not talking about the two of you vocally. I'm talking about your energy onstage. You draw people to you—to the two of you. I can't believe you haven't been singing together this whole time."

"Rory wanted an opera career. Then she taught for a while. She only just recently devoted herself to rock and roll."

Derek looks toward Rory, his gaze sliding over her in that way I don't like. "She's amazing. Her voice is like...almost surreal. The closest I can think of to compare her to is maybe Karen Carpenter in her early days. A lower voice for a woman, but an amazing range."

"That's Rory's classical training," I say, willing myself to stay cool.

"Yeah, but... I hate to even say this because Karen Carpenter was an amazing talent, but Rory's better. Karen Carpenter never could have *rocked*. Rory rocks. She's right up there with those female rockers of the seventies and eighties. Annie Lennox, Ann Wilson, Chrissie Hynde. She's fucking fabulous."

"You don't have to sell me on my sister. Vocally, she's more talented than I am."

"I wouldn't say that. Because the two of you... You just mesh. Your sound is a raspy baritone, which is what makes you unique. Most rockers are in the tenor range."

"Jett's not."

"No, he's not. That's why Emerald Phoenix climbed up the charts so fast. Jett has a unique sound for a rocker. He gives it a rich low timbre. And you do the same, except you can go a little higher than he goes."

"Thank you for the compliment. I appreciate it." And I do. Maybe Derek isn't a bad guy after all. Perhaps I'm being too hard on him.

"I'm not even close to joshing you. I swear to God, I think your band is going places. And damn..." He leans in and lowers his voice. "If you choose to give your drummer the boot for this little fiasco he pulled? I'll always be there to have your back."

An angry crow pecks at my neck. He didn't just insinuate that we were going to dump Dragon, did he?

Yeah, he did. Seems my original feelings about him were right on target.

But I have a smile on my face anyway. Because truth be told, this guy saved our asses tonight, and he played like a dream.

"That's good to know, Derek. I appreciate it." *In your dreams*, I add silently.

"Anytime. I look forward to playing with you guys again in Edinburgh."

Emerald Phoenix takes the stage then, and I sit with Rory and Brock. The band rocks like hell, of course. And when the concert is over, they do not one, not two, but three encores.

Then we all head to the backstage area, where—of course—groupies galore are congregating.

I spy Maddie and head straight to her side. I'm not letting her out of my sight.

"What did you think?" I ask.

A wide grin splits Maddie's pretty face. "You and Rory were even more amazing than you were last night. And your drummer's good, Jess."

"Yeah, he's pretty amazing. I can't believe Jett let us use him. He could've so easily screwed us all over. Claimed breach of contract."

"Surely your contract has some kind of provision if one of you can't perform. People get sick."

"Of course it does. But it also means we don't get paid for that concert. And drug ODs are specifically excluded."

"They are?"

"Hell yeah," I say. "Donny and Callie went through that thing with a fine-tooth comb, made sure the rest of the band and I understood exactly what we were signing."

Funny, with my little sister on my arm, the groupies stay away from me like I'm poison.

Just as well.

After what happened with Dragon? I'm staying the hell away from these women. I already promised Rory. And myself.

Besides...

Only one woman makes me feel like I've never felt before.

And she's at the hospital, at Dragon's bedside.

I let my adrenaline pump through me, sang my heart out, made sure I gave the crowd a concert worth remembering.

But then, when our set was over, and my high started to slow down... I looked in the front row.

And I saw Maddie. Donny and Callie. Brock.

But no Brianna.

And a little piece of my heart died.

CHAPTER TEN

Brianna

My neck is killing me, my back hurts, and I haven't had a good night's sleep.

Of course I haven't. I slept in a chair, next to Dragon's bed in the hospital ward.

But I promised Jesse I wouldn't leave his side, and I don't plan to.

When I open my eyes and stretch, I find Dragon is awake, his hazel eyes wide open.

"When the hell can I get out of here?"

"I don't know, Dragon," I say. "Your doctor hasn't been by yet this morning."

He squints at me. "When did you get here?"

"I never left."

"Oh fuck..." he says. "The concert. What happened with the concert?"

I'm not sure what to do to assuage him. Pat his shoulder? I hardly know him. I reach toward him and then think better of it. No touching. "I got a text from Maddie. She said it was fantastic. The backup drummer was great. So everything's fine. You don't need to worry."

"Yeah, I do." He rubs at his eyes. "I may have just lost my job."

"No, we've got it all figured out," I say. "You're going to stay here until your doctor releases you, which may be later today. And then you'll stay at the hotel in London while the band travels to Edinburgh and Glasgow, and then back to London."

"And they'll be using the other drummer?"

"Yeah. So you can take some time to rest and recuperate. I'll be staying with you."

"Scratch that," a voice says from behind me.

My brother's voice.

Donny and Callie are here.

"Hey." A giant yawn splits my face. "What are you guys doing here?"

"Callie and I just talked to Dragon's doctor, and he's being released today. We decided we don't want you to miss the rest of the tour."

I wipe the sleep out of my tired eyes. "What do you mean?"

"He means," Callie says, "that Donny and I are going to stay here in London at the hotel with Dragon. Make sure he has everything he needs." She walks to me and touches my shoulder lightly. "You and Maddie came so that you could experience Europe together. I don't want to take that away from my sister or you."

It's all making sense to me now. They're more concerned about Maddie's experience than mine. Maddie is Callie's sister, though, and she did put off her last semester of college. And part of that deal was traveling with me.

"But..."

"No buts, sis," Donny says. "Callie and I can come back to the UK anytime. And this way, we can spend some more time with Ennis Ainsley. We'd both like to get to know him better. In fact, believe it or not, I talked to Dale on the phone, and he and

Ashley are taking a few days off to come to London to meet us here and spend time with Ennis."

"So I'm missing my brother?"

"You'll see him when the band gets back to London. He and Ashley will stay for the concert and then a few days more after the band leaves for Paris." Donny shakes his head, chuckling. "Callie and I want to do this for you. And Ennis really wants to meet with Dale and talk wine. It's all working out."

I cross my arms. My brother's right. It's all working out for the best, but I'm exhausted and I'm feeling petulant. "Maybe I'd like to see Ennis again too."

"Then you can. Callie and I are having lunch with him today. I'd love for you to join us."

I stretch, rubbing my neck. "I need a shower."

Donny holds his nose. "Yeah, you sure do."

I want to stand and swat him, but it's too much effort.

"You need some rest too," he continues. "Go on back to the hotel. Callie and I will stay here with Dragon until he's released, which should be before lunchtime, according to his doctor."

"All right. But I hate that you're missing out on your trip."

He smiles. "Remember, our trip was only for the UK portion anyway. Callie and I will come back and see Edinburgh. Or maybe we'll stay with Dale and Ashley after Dragon and the band set course for Paris. Nothing is stopping us from staying."

"Except for your jobs," I say.

"All I need to do is call Mom. She's running the show now, and she won't mind running it for another few days."

That much is true. Donny is our mother's Achilles' heel. She and he have a bond the rest of us don't share with her.

"If the two of you are sure," I say.

"Absolutely," Callie says, smiling. "This is what's best for us and for you and Maddie. Donny and I have seen two concerts, one with Dragon and one without. We're good."

I give my brother a quick hug and kiss him on the cheek. "You're awesome," I say.

Donny wipes his cheek where I kissed him. "Don't you forget it. Now get out of here, grab a cab, go back to the hotel, and shower, and see if you can get a few hours of rest. Then, I want you to meet Callie and me at The Old Bank of England on Fleet Street at one p.m. That's where we're meeting Ennis for lunch. Be sure to try the priest."

As tired as I am, I laugh at my brother. Donny can always make me laugh.

★ ★ ★

After a shower, a few hours of quick sleep, and a pot of lovely English tea, I take a cab and exit in front of The Old Bank of England on Fleet Street. Another gorgeous building that I wish Diana were here to see, but since I know nothing about architecture and I'm starving, I don't take the time to memorize any more details. I walk into the restaurant.

Dark paneling and brass fixtures adorn the dining room. On the walls are historical artwork, photographs, and memorabilia related to Fleet Street's history as a center of journalism and publishing. A full bar stands to one side, and the seating options are varied and include wooden tables and cozy booths.

I spy Donny, Callie, and Ennis at a table near the back.

"I see my party," I say to the hostess.

"Brilliant. Go on back, then."

"Ms. Steel," Ennis says, "so lovely to see you once again."

I shake his outstretched hand. "Please, you knew me when I was a baby. Call me Brianna. Or Bree."

"Then you must call me Ennis."

He and Donny both rise, and Ennis holds a chair for me.

Callie's holding the list of alcoholic beverages, and she hands it to Ennis. "You know way more than I do about this kind of stuff."

Ennis stares at her hand.

"That's a lovely ring."

"Yes, isn't it?"

"I noticed it when you were at my house for tea the other day, but I didn't get this good a look at it. May I?"

Callie holds her left hand out, and Ennis takes it, eyeing the ring.

"May I ask where you got this?" he asks Donny.

Donny nods. "It's actually a copy of a ring that used to belong to my mother. We haven't been able to ascertain where the original came from."

Ennis closes his eyes. "I never dared hope."

"Hope what?" Callie asks.

"You still have the original, then? I'd heard it had been stolen."

"Yes, it's in my father's safe," Donny says.

"It has the initials LW inside," Callie says. "Donny and his parents haven't been able to figure out where it came from or why Daphne even had it."

"Yeah," Donny says. "My grandmother's—Daphne's mother's—initials were LW. Lucy Wade. But she came from a modest background, and she never would've been able to afford a ring like this. It's a fire diamond, and it's priceless."

"Yes, I know."

Donny cocks his head. "How do you know about it?"

"Because I'm the one who gave it to Daphne."

CHAPTER ELEVEN

Jesse

I tossed and turned all night in the room next to Brock and Rory's suite, and when I finally did get some sleep, Brianna haunted my dreams.

Every song I've ever written went through my mind, and somehow I found a way to relate every one of them to Brianna Steel.

My thoughts and feelings have taken me over—and frankly, they're disturbing.

By the time I get up and take a shower, it's nearly noon. We're taking a late train to Edinburgh tonight, and I can't stand the thought of leaving Dragon here.

But he's not ready to do the concerts yet, so we're going to leave him here. He'll be released to the hotel, and apparently Brianna and Maddie will be staying there.

I made arrangements to meet Brock and Rory for lunch to go over everything from here on out until Dragon can return to the tour when we head across the English Channel to Paris. Then I'll have a little time to go see Dragon in the hospital before we leave for Edinburgh.

I hurry to the restaurant, making it just in time. Brock and Rory are already sitting at a table.

"I was just about to text you," Rory says.

I yawn. "I overslept. It took a while for me to get to sleep, so I needed it."

"You're good. No rehearsal or concert today."

I've always been the de facto leader of our band, but now that Rory has officially joined, she has taken charge. Funny, Rory always wanted to be a mother. It's been her dream since she was a little girl.

Now she's kind of acting as the mother for the band.

Honestly? I don't have a huge problem with that. If she wants to take over leading, I'm good. She knows as much about music as I do, in some ways more.

"So," I say, perusing the menu. "What are we going to do about Maddie? She was looking forward to seeing all of the UK."

"Oh, right," Brock says. "You don't know yet."

I lift my eyebrows. "Know what?"

"Donny and Callie have volunteered to stay here in London at the hotel with Dragon once he's released. So Maddie and Brianna can continue on the tour with us."

"Oh."

I'm not sure how to feel.

I want what's best for my sister—and she is putting off her last semester of college for this. I want her to be able to see the rest of our tour in the UK.

"Did they volunteer?"

"Yeah," Rory says. "It was Callie's idea, actually. She and Donny can come back and see the UK whenever they want, and this may be the only time Maddie gets the chance. So she didn't want to take this experience away from her."

Part of me jumps for joy at the idea that Brianna's going to be with us for the rest of the UK tour.

Part of me dreads it.

I can't be distracted.

But I can handle that. I can force Brianna out of my mind and do a good concert. I've proved that. But having her there— casually seeing her...

Constantly wanting her...

Her presence will make it all so much more difficult.

"Isn't it great?" Rory says. "Everything has worked out."

"Yeah, I suppose so," I say.

She narrows her eyes toward me. "You don't sound too excited."

"Well, I think it was Brianna who volunteered to stay with Dragon."

"She did," Brock says, "but she also promised Maddie a wonderful experience. Something they could do together. So Callie decided, for Maddie's sake, that Brianna should be with Maddie on this trip."

It all makes sense, of course. Everyone's thinking of our youngest sibling, and in truth, I get it.

"Jess?" Rory says. "Do you have an issue with this?"

I blink. "Of course not."

"Good. Because it seems to solve all our problems."

I shake my head. "All our problems? Our drummer's in the hospital."

"Yes, he is. He screwed up. But we've fixed it. We've got Derek as a backup drummer, and he's fabulous. You said so yourself."

I nod, saying nothing. No need to tell Rory of my doubts about Derek. I'm probably freaking out over nothing. So he runs his mouth off and says things he shouldn't. Who doesn't sometimes?

Rory pats my shoulder. "It's not optimal. But we've got things fixed, Jess. The tour is going on as planned, and Dragon will meet up with us in Paris."

"I know."

"He may even be able to do the final concert in London once we get back here," Rory says.

I look to the floor. "Yeah, I hope so."

"If he can't, we'll use Derek."

"Right." I scan the menu.

Derek. The lifesaver. The guy who hates addicts. The guy who'd have my sister in the sack in a minute if he could finagle it.

Brock rises. "Excuse me. I've got to see a man about a horse." He leaves the table.

"Brock ordered for us," Rory says. "Traditional English breakfast."

I slam my menu down on the table. "Maybe I don't *want* the traditional English breakfast today. Did anyone ever think of that?"

Rory's eyes go wide. "It's what you've eaten every day since you've been here," Rory says. "I just thought—"

"I am so tired of other people thinking for me. Making decisions for me."

"Jess," Rory says. "No one ever makes decisions for you. Where the hell is this coming from?"

I rise, rake my fingers through my hair, and then I plunk back in my seat.

Energy is sizzling through me. And those crows are pecking at the back of my neck again.

I'm angry. There's no reason to be angry. Rory and Brock are right. Everything has worked out perfectly. More perfectly than we could've ever planned, given Dragon's mishap.

And then I realize it's not anger that I'm feeling.

No, it's something much deeper, something that is inflaming my body.

It's passion.

Angry passion, and I don't want to have it.

And now...

Now Brianna will be with us.

Which is okay.

I can handle it.

I have to.

"Traditional English breakfast is fine. Black tea."

"It's on its way," Rory says. "Now, do you want to tell me what that outburst was about?"

"Just everything," I say.

"Yes, I know what happened to Dragon was horrible. But we have to look on the bright side, Jesse. He's going to be okay. We found a replacement for the next several concerts. And if Dragon needs to go to rehab, we'll keep Derek for the entire tour."

"No," I say adamantly. "I want Dragon. He's a member of this band, Rory. We don't turn our back on our own. He's been with the band a long time."

Rory draws in a breath, lets it out slowly. "And I haven't. Is that what you're getting at?"

"No... Yes..." I run my fingers through my hair again. "I don't know, Ror. Give me a fucking break, okay?"

"What exactly is going on here?" Brock asks when he returns to the table.

"This is band business, Steel."

"Wait, wait, wait..." Rory shakes her head at me. "Brock

is my fiancé, and he's a financier of our part of the store. You won't talk to him like that."

She's right, of course. I'm being a dickhead, and I know it. "I'm sorry," I murmur.

Rory shakes her head at me.

Dragon...

Why did Dragon have to fuck up?

Why did I have to sleep with Brianna Steel?

She's inside me now, like a fucking virus I can't shake. Or like a poison for which there's no antidote. A poison that both gives me life and takes it from me with each dose.

And it's eating at me. Eating at me, clawing at my heart.

The server comes with our tea, and I take a quick sip. The tea burns my tongue.

"Damn," I say.

"Jesse," Rory says, "you've got to calm down. We're all sorry about what happened to Dragon. But everything has fallen into place better than any of us could've imagined. We still have the chance to make a name for ourselves on this tour."

"Dragon should be part of it."

"Yes, he should. But he's not. Whether he was drugged or he took the drugs himself, the result is the same. Things couldn't have worked out better."

Things *could've* worked out better. Brianna could be staying here with Dragon. But then Maddie wouldn't have anyone to experience the tour with...

Rory's right. I don't know why I'm being so obstinate.

Except I do know.

Because as long as Brianna Steel is on this trip, I will continue to be distracted. I can try to force her out of my head. I can focus and perform and do a great job.

But having her here will make it just a little bit more difficult.

And now, without Dragon, I don't need anything making this more difficult.

I stir my tea, helping it cool, and then I take another sip.

I look my sister in the eye. "Thank you, Ror. Thank you for maintaining a cool head through this. I promise you that from now on, I will be completely focused on every part of this tour."

CHAPTER TWELVE

Brianna

My jaw nearly drops onto the table. "You gave the ring to my grandmother?"

"We've had it appraised," Donny says. "It's priceless."

Ennis nods. "I know. My mum gave it to me. It belonged to her grandmother, who came from Australia. Her name was Lottie Walsh."

"I'm sure you had a very good reason," Donny continues, "but I have to ask. Why would you give a priceless heirloom to our grandmother?"

Ennis stares into space for a moment, and just when I'm not sure he's going to say another word—

"I haven't brought those memories to the surface in quite some time," he says. "But I suppose you deserve to know the truth about where the ring came from."

"Yes, please," I say. "I'm sure it's a story of true love."

Ennis's eyes mist a little. "It is, dear Brianna. It is."

"Then tell us," I plead. I want to hear Ennis's story since my own story of true love clearly isn't going to happen.

"Patty was the daughter of pig farmers," Ennis says, "but such a humble background didn't matter to me. When we found out Daphne's first pregnancy—with your uncle Jonah—had been difficult, we were surprised. Patty was taken aback because she and Daphne were quite close. We were visiting Daphne, and of course the subject of Sean Murphy came up. Did you know Patty dated him before me?"

"Jack's father?" I ask.

"Yes, the one who died at Brad and Daphne's wedding." He sighs. "I was in love with Patty from our first encounter, but she held a torch for Sean. Once he died, I wasn't sure Patty would fall for me." A smile spreads over his still-handsome face. "But she did." Then he goes dark. "I suppose I knew something wasn't right, though I had no idea Patty might be a victim, when we had dinner with your grandparents the next night."

I watch Ennis then, how his blue eyes sparkle with both happiness and sadness as he brings the memories to the surface.

And when he speaks, his words turn into images before me.

Ennis

"Miss Daphne," Belinda, the housekeeper, interrupted. "Phone for you. It's Mr. Brad."

Daphne rose from the dinner table, which included both her mother and mother-in-law, plus Patty and me.

Daphne returned a few moments later. "Brad is staying in the city tonight. Says he has an early meeting. But he promises he'll be home for dinner tomorrow night, so you guys need to come back."

Patty nodded. "Sure. Is that okay with you, Ennis?"

"Yeah, of course, love," I said. "This beef is fantastic. Even better than at your wedding."

"It's filet," Daphne said, "and Belinda broils it to perfection."

"It's truly amazing," Lucy, Daphne's mother, agreed. "I wish we could get this kind of beef in Denver."

"I'll send a full cooler home with you," Daphne said. "And we'll send you as much as you want after that."

"My daughter, the beef queen!" Lucy laughed.

"Mistress of Steel Acres!" Patty raised her wineglass. "Did you ever think, Daph, when we met last fall, that you'd be here, with a gorgeous little boy, less than a year later?"

"God, no," Daphne said, "but I wouldn't change a thing."

"You're so lucky," Patty gushed, tossing her fiery red hair over her shoulders.

God, she was beautiful. Already I'd fallen hard. But she might still be hung up on Sean Murphy...even though he was no competition at this point, having died at Brad and Daphne's wedding.

Daphne jerked when the doorbell rang.

"I'll get it!" Belinda called.

A few minutes passed as we all continued eating.

"Telegram for you, Miss Daphne." Belinda strode in and handed Daphne a yellow envelope.

"A telegram?" Mazie, Brad's mother, shook her head. "Do people still send telegrams?"

"My parents got one when I was a kid," Lucy said. "That's the last I remember."

Daphne held the yellow envelope from Western Union. "It's already open."

"I thought they stopped sending these a few years ago," Belinda said.

"Who delivered it?" Daphne asked.

"Just a kid. I didn't recognize him."

"Was he wearing anything that said Western Union on it?" Mazie asked.

"No. He looked about sixteen or so."

Daphne pulled out a folded piece of paper. It was plain white.

"It should be yellow," Lucy said, "to match the envelope."

"You're right, Lucy," Mazie agreed. "I don't think that's a telegram at all. It's a message using an old Western Union envelope."

Daphne unfolded the paper.

Her face went pale, and her lips trembled. My heart nearly stopped. What did that paper say?

"Daphne, you're white as a sheet," Lucy said. "What is it?"

Her hands shook.

"Daphne?" Lucy said again.

"What is it, dear?" Mazie that time.

Finally, Patty grabbed the paper from her hand. She glanced at it, and her mouth dropped open. "Who sent this?" she finally said.

Daphne didn't answer.

"What's it say?" I asked, my skin going cold.

Patty handed it to me, and my flesh went colder.

Keep that baby close. Wouldn't want anything to happen to him.

Brianna

I gulp. "Uncle Joe?"

Ennis nods. "That should have been my first clue to keep my eye on Patty and Daphne. Obviously your uncle was never harmed, but he was just an infant. Anyone who would threaten an infant..."

I feel sick. How much more has my family kept from all of us? Or do they even know this story?

"We were supposed to go back to Brad and Daphne's place for dinner the next night," Ennis goes on, "but that never happened."

Ennis

I wasn't sure I should bother Daphne after the frightening message she received the previous evening, but I was getting worried. We were supposed to go back to Brad and Daphne's for dinner, but Patty had gone out shopping, and she hadn't returned yet. The last thing I wanted to do was worry Daphne further, but she was expecting us.

I dialed her and forced myself to sound cheerful. "Hey, love. Patty's not back from shopping yet, so we may be late for dinner."

"Wow. Is it dinnertime already?" she asked.

"We're due at your place in a half hour, which means we need to leave now. She took off after lunch to shop."

"Snow Creek isn't that big."

That thought had also crossed my mind. Snow Creek is tiny. How much shopping was there to do? An antique place, an old-style five-and-dime, a tattoo parlor, a vintage clothing store, a dress shop, and a shoe store. Patty could browse for hours, but this was getting ridiculous.

And given Sean Murphy's recent demise and the eerie threat against baby Joe last night... Something was clawing at the back of my neck.

And I didn't like it.

Again I forced cheer into my voice. "You know Patty. She's got the shopping bug. I expected her back at the hotel by now."

"I'll tell Belinda you might be a little late," she said. "Let me know when you're on your way."

"Will do. Thanks for understanding."

"Patty dragged me out shopping a couple of days after I first met her. She's a born shopper. See you soon."

Time passed slowly. I watched the clock on our hotel room nightstand flip each minute. I paced the small room until I was certain I'd worn out the carpeting. A half hour passed. Then an hour.

I called Daphne again, and this time I couldn't force cheer into my voice.

"She's still not back, love. I'm going out to look for her."

"Ennis, you don't know the town. Let me come help you."

"No!" I nearly shout. "You stay with the baby. If something happened to him, I'd never forgive myself. Please."

"Yes." She pauses. "Yes, of course. You're right. Please keep me posted."

"I will."

I left the hotel and walked around the main area of the small Colorado town. It was after seven by this time, and most of the shops had closed. The tattoo parlor was still open, so I went in there.

"Good evening," a heavily tattooed young man with a septum piercing said. "You got an appointment?"

"No, sir. I'm looking for my girlfriend. Her name's Patty, and she left me to shop here in town right after lunch. Red hair, gorgeous. You can't miss her."

"Haven't seen anyone like that. Sorry."

Fear sliced through me as I left the tattoo place. Most of the shops seemed to be small and locally owned, so I went to each one and pounded on each door. Only one person came to the door at the shoe store.

"We're closed," she said through the glass.

"Are you Mariah?" I asked, glancing at the sign, *Mariah's Shoes and Stuff.*

"Yeah."

"Sorry to bother you, but I'm looking for my girlfriend. She was shopping here before. Red hair, beautiful, bright personality? Loves shoes?"

"Look, Mister..."

"Ainsley. Ennis Ainsley."

"Mr. Ainsley, you're obviously not from here with the accent and all, but Snow Creek is about as safe a place as there is. She may have run off."

I turned stone cold.

Was it possible? Could Patty not be feeling for me what I was feeling for her?

Could she—

But we'd had an amazing morning. Best sex I'd ever had, and she'd said it was the same for her. We'd exchanged *I love yous* and everything.

"No." I shook my head vehemently. "Absolutely not. Have you seen her?"

"I don't recall seeing a redhead in here." She shifted her gaze around nervously. "Look, I've got to get supper on for the kids. I'm sorry I can't help you."

What was I missing? I went in all the restaurants and looked for her. She wouldn't be in a restaurant. She would never miss dinner with Daphne and Brad.

Which told me all I needed to know.

She couldn't have run off on me. She wouldn't do that to me. She wouldn't do that to Daphne.

With nowhere else to look, I just walked up and down the street, gazing into dark windows, hoping against hope I'd see her beautiful freckled face.

I jerked when a hand gripped my shoulder from behind.

"Ennis."

I turned and stared into the dark eyes of Brad Steel.

"I've checked everywhere," I said before he even spoke. "It's like she disappeared into thin air."

"Have you called her parents? Maybe she..."

"Took off?" I shook my head. Why was everyone saying that? "I already thought of that. But after the morning we had, I doubt it."

"Good sex?"

"Better than good. And we said *I love you* for the first time."

"You think she got cold feet?"

"No. Plus, Patty isn't one to mince words. If she wanted to leave me, she would have told me."

Brad nodded. "I don't like this."

"Neither do I, mate." A chill ran down my spine. "I'm worried. Really worried."

"The cops are on it. I called them. Have you seen them wandering around?"

"Honestly, I haven't noticed. I've only been looking for red hair."

"I get it. They're going to want to talk to you."

"Hey, wait." I lowered my eyelids. "You don't think..."

"I don't know. But like you say, Patty wouldn't just leave."

I regarded Brad Steel—his swarthy good looks and dark

eyes. The man who'd charmed Daphne Wade. He was rich beyond my wildest dreams, but something wasn't right. A man had dropped dead at his wedding, and someone was threatening an innocent infant—his son.

If I squinted, I could almost see a shadow of evil following him.

"Steel, I'm beginning to regret the day I ever laid eyes on you."

I expected him to react, but he said nothing.

And I started to feel bad about what I said. I was imagining things. A shadow of evil? Come on.

"Look," I began. "I didn't mean—"

"Yeah, you did."

Well, if he agreed... "Okay, I did. What the hell is going on?"

"I'd tell you if I knew."

"You've got to know someone who has it out for you."

He was quiet for a moment, until—

"I'm working on it," he said.

This time I curled my hands into fists. All the fear in my heart turned to anger toward Brad. "Steel, you've got to do better than that. The woman I love is—"

"I know. I'll do what I can." He shook his head. "This will kill Daphne."

I adored Daphne, but they were friends. Patty and I were partners, lovers. "Not as much as it will kill me. We were talking about going to London to meet my folks. Then touring the continent."

"I know, man. I'm sorry." He touched my shoulder lightly. "You're right. It will affect you worse. I'm walking over to the police station to file the report. You want to come along?

They'll need to talk to you anyway."

I didn't respond, simply nodded.

We walked in silence the few blocks to the station, and I answered their questions as best I could. I knew very little.

"You'll stay with us for now," Brad said to me. "At least I know you'll be safe. I've got round-the-clock security since Joe was threatened."

I didn't say anything. Simply nodded again, and then we went to the hotel, and I packed up all Patty's and my belongings. Daphne was awake when we got to their place.

"Ennis is staying with us now," Brad said.

"Patty?" Daphne asked, wide-eyed.

"She's missing," I said.

"No..."

"Not officially until twenty-four hours have passed," Brad said.

"Not officially?" Daphne asked. "You think that makes a difference?"

"No, baby, I don't. Ennis and I have been talking to the cops for the last couple of hours. They've checked every shop in Snow Creek and even went around the residences in town and knocked on doors. Patty's gone."

"And no one saw her?"

"Not that we've found yet." He caressed Daphne's cheek. "I'm so sorry, baby."

"No, just no." She laid Joe in his bassinet. "This can't be happening."

My eyes glazed over, and I had to hold back the tears. "It is, love. I wish it weren't, but it is."

"But how...?"

"We'll find her," Brad said. "I asked you to trust me."

"I do trust you, but so did Patty." Daphne swallowed. "So did Sean."

Brad's facial muscles went rigid. They were about to quarrel, and I needed an exit strategy.

"You should get to bed," Brad said to me.

"Why? I won't be able to sleep." I paced around, my nerves a jumbling mass. "Besides...I'm going to have to call her parents."

"That can wait until morning," Brad said.

"If your child were missing, would you want to wait until morning to find out?" I turned to leave the room.

"Wait!" Daphne's eyebrows shot up. "Maybe they know where she is. Maybe she went home."

"She's not," Brad said. "I already called them earlier this evening and posed as a friend from school. They haven't heard from her. If she'd flown home, she'd have called them with the information."

"Maybe not. Maybe she wanted to surprise them."

"There's one way to find out," I said. "I'm calling them."

"Use my office," Brad said. "You want me to come along?"

"No, I'll do it alone. I just wish I knew what the hell to say."

"Wait, Ennis," Daphne said. "Don't call them."

"I have to, Daphne."

"But she's... She's not..."

"She's missing, love. They're her parents. They have a right to know."

"No, Brad. Please."

"He's right, baby. He has to make this phone call."

"No. No. No." Her voice sounded oddly robotic as I left the room.

I found Brad's office. Myriad papers were scattered across his desk. Should I look at them? Maybe find clues?

But in my heart, I knew Brad had nothing to do with Patty's disappearance. He'd never do anything to harm Daphne. He loved Daphne, and Daphne loved Patty.

I dialed the number for Patty's parents in Iowa.

What would I say to them? I didn't know, so I winged it.

"Hello?"

"Mr. Watson?"

A throat cleared. "Yes. This is he."

"It's Ennis Ainsley in Colorado."

"Of course, Patty's friend. How are you?"

"Not good at all, I'm afraid." This time I cleared my throat. "I don't know how to tell you this, but I'm in Snow Creek with Brad and Daphne Steel, friends of Patty's."

"I see." His voice sounded fearful.

I swallowed. "Patty is... That is... She's gone. Disappeared. We can't find her."

Silence for a moment, until, "Excuse me?"

"I'm so sorry. We've called the police, and you know Bradford Steel has a lot of money. I'm sure we'll find her, Mr. Watson."

"What have you done?" he roared.

"I haven't done anything." Tears welled in my eyes. "She went shopping, and she didn't come back."

"You let her go alone?"

"I..." I didn't know what to say. Yes, I'd let her go alone. She was a grown woman in a small town. But guilt ate away at my guts like a parasite.

"I'm calling the police in Snow Creek."

"Yes. Yes, of course. You should do that. They're looking into this."

He slammed the phone down so hard that I jerked at the

echo in my ear.

I numbly stumbled out of Brad's office and to the guest room where he'd put my things.

The next day passed in a haze. I couldn't tell you what I did, who I talked to. All I could think about was Patty. Was she hurt? Struggling? Every horrid thing that could be happening to her went through my head in excruciating detail.

Two days later, I received a phone call from Mr. Watson.

"Ennis, I'm sorry to have to tell you this, but Patty has left the country. She called her mother and me a few hours ago from Togo, Africa." He draws in a breath so harshly I can hear it through the phone. "She joined the Peace Corps. I'm sorry."

No.

What?

I went numb once more.

Patty left me? After she said she loved me? The Peace Corps? A noble calling, but she'd only finished one year of college.

Never once did Patty mention any desire to join the Peace Corps.

"Excuse me?" I finally say.

He clears his throat and then clears it again. "Yes, it was a surprise to us as well. Especially that she didn't say goodbye before she left. But Patty can be prone to impulsive decisions, Ennis. I'm sorry."

"But—"

He hung up the phone.

And I stared into space for what seemed like forever.

I said a quick goodbye to Brad, Daphne, and the baby the next day and traveled back to London.

Brianna

"How did my grandmother end up with your ring, then?" I ask.

"The story's far from over." He sighs. "I never believed Patty had left me to join the Peace Corps. To this day, I have no idea why her father told me she did."

Donny shakes his head. "I'd bet Wendy Madigan had a hand in that."

"Perhaps," Ennis says, "since we finally know for sure that Wendy Madigan had Patty killed." He closes his eyes. "Sometimes I still can't believe it, but it gives me a sense of peace to finally know she didn't leave me willingly."

"But the ring..." I insist.

"Easy, Bree," my brother says.

"It's all right," Ennis says. "A few months later, I had a horrid dream about Patty. I can't recall the details—I couldn't then, even though it caused me to wake up in a cold sweat—but the gist was that something terrible had happened to Patty in Colorado."

"Which it did," I say.

"Yes, though I didn't know that at the time. But I felt I had to investigate, so I returned to Colorado...and this time, I took the ring."

"For Patty?"

"Yes. If I found her, I was going to slip it on her finger and never let her go." He chuckles softly. "I never did like the ring, but the color...just like Patty's hair. It's like it had been mined specifically for her." He closes his eyes.

Ennis

I returned to the same hotel—the only one in Snow Creek—and was walking around town, still feeling a profound loss, when I saw Daphne exit the small medical building.

"Daphne, love?"

She turned and ran into my arms. "Ennis! What are you doing here?"

"Just walking around town a bit. I had no idea you were here."

Daphne broke the embrace. "Why didn't you tell me you were coming to town!"

"I didn't know I was until two days ago. It was a rash decision."

"Oh. Is everything okay?"

"I had a nightmare about Patty, and I had to come."

"Patty? I figured she was still in Africa."

"She is, as far as I know. But I had this horrid dream about her. That something terrible had happened. Here. In Colorado."

"I'm so sorry. But why would that make you want to come all the way out here? Not that I'm sorry. It's wonderful to see you. You should stay with us on the ranch."

"That's kind of you, but I've already booked a room at the hotel. The same room Patty and I stayed in when..."

"Oh. That's an eerie coincidence."

"Actually, I requested it."

"Why would you do that?"

A chill raced up my neck. I had no answer for her. "I don't know. I just did. I said the words before I thought about them."

"Are you still in love with her, Ennis?"

I nodded. "It's only been a little over three months. I've tried getting over her. Tried telling myself that she left me. That leaving her home was more important than I was. I can't fault her. The Peace Corps is amazing. But she never once mentioned the thought to me. I've always thought it strange that she just left without saying anything to anyone. Especially not to me or to you. So when I had the dream, I couldn't help but be freaked out by it."

"It was just a dream, Ennis."

"I know that, love. But haven't you ever had a dream that spoke to you? That felt so damned real you could almost feel it?"

She nodded. "Yeah. I have, actually."

"Then you know what I mean."

"What do you plan to do while you're here?"

"I'm not sure. I haven't thought it out yet. I just knew, after that dream, that I had to come."

"I'm on my way back to the ranch now. You won't believe how big Jonah is. You should come and stay for dinner."

"I was going to call you this afternoon," I said. "Running into you is so much better. I was hoping..."

"Hoping what?"

"That Brad might be able to help. I want to hire a private investigator. I'm just not sure Patty's actually in Africa."

"Ennis, you know I adore you, and I know you adored Patty, but her parents told you she called them from Africa, remember?"

I nodded. "Of course I remember. I just have this eerie feeling. I swear, if a PI tells me she's definitely in Africa, I'll call it all off."

"Come for dinner at six, okay? Or you can come home with me now."

I considered her request, but what I truly wanted was to talk to Brad. Other than that, small talk sounded like torture.

"I'll be there at six," I told her. "I've rented a car, so I have my own transport."

The hours passed slowly in the hotel room, and when five o'clock arrived, I got into my rental and drove to the house in Steel Acres.

Turned out Brad was late for dinner, and Daphne asked Belinda to hold it for a half hour for him. She and I sat together in her large family room.

"Have you thought about talking to anyone about the dream?" she asked me.

"I just had the dream a couple of nights ago. I haven't been able to think about anything other than getting here and investigating."

"I just meant..." She cleared her throat. "I work with a psychiatrist. Dr. Pelletier. He's been a big help to me."

"I'm sorry, love. What are you struggling with?"

"He's helping me deal with what happened to my mother. I've had some anxiety and depression, and I don't want it to affect the baby."

"Of course. And he's helping you?"

She nodded. "He is."

"Honestly, this is the first time I've had a dream that seemed so real. I don't think I need counseling. I just needed to come here and make sure it wasn't true."

"I understand."

Brad walked into the kitchen then and opened the French doors. Their dogs, Ebony and Brandy, ran in.

Daphne stood. "Looks like it's time for dinner."

I followed her into the kitchen. Belinda had set the table

on the deck out back.

"Hey," Daphne said to Brad. "We have company for dinner."

Brad looked up from the dogs. "Oh? Hey, Ennis."

"Hope you don't mind me barging in."

"Not at all. When did you get back in the States?"

"Just this morning, actually."

"Good to see you. I'm going to wash up. You two go ahead and start. Mom's already out there. Thanks for holding dinner for me." He leaned down and brushed his lips across Daphne's.

"No problem."

Daphne and I joined Mazie on the deck. We made some small talk until Brad arrived.

Belinda's dinner was delicious, but the conversation was mundane. Brad was quiet, and so was I.

Then, Brad, to my astonishment, turned to me. "What are you really doing here?"

I widened my eyes.

"No offense, man," Brad continued, "but no one packs up and heads over the Atlantic without letting their friends know they're coming. Unless they left quickly."

"Brad..." Daphne said.

"It's okay, Daph." I forced out a chuckle. "We both know he's right."

Brad's facial muscles didn't move as I told him about the dream. Completely immobile. Oddly immobile. As if he were forcing his expression to remain the same.

"I understand why you'd be upset by the nightmare," Brad said. "But Patty's parents are the ones who told us she'd decided to join the Peace Corps."

"I know that. But isn't it strange that she just left? Didn't bother telling any of us? We'd just declared our love for each other, for God's sake."

"It does seem strange," Daphne said. "But she's not the first friend to leave me and never communicate with me again. It happened to me in high school. By my best friend Sage Peterson."

"And that doesn't strike you as odd that it's happened twice?" I asked her.

"If it's happened twice," Daphne said, "maybe it's normal. I don't know."

Odd, really, the way she put that. As if having best friends disappear on you is a normal thing. No wonder she was seeing a psychiatrist. Was Daphne all right? She didn't look ill, but mental illness doesn't always show itself.

"I'll tell you what," Brad said. "Since you came all the way here, I'll make some phone calls. I have contacts just about everywhere. Someone must know someone at the Peace Corps. I'll try to get confirmation that Patty's working with them."

I nodded eagerly. "That would be great, Brad. Thank you."

"No problem. Always happy to help out a friend." Brad stood. "Either of you care for an after-dinner drink?"

"Not while I'm nursing," Daphne said.

"Sure. Anything's fine with me," I said.

Brad left and returned a few minutes later with two bourbons. "I don't have any decent wine in the house. I'm looking to hire a vintner. Our vineyards bloomed in spring, and we're expecting a hell of a harvest. My father had a top-scale wine-producing facility built on the east quadrant a year and a half ago. If I don't find someone soon, I'll have to arrange to sell our grapes to another winery."

"I know a little about wine," I said.

"You do?" Brad lifted his eyebrows.

"Sounds strange, huh? A Brit who knows about wine?" I chuckled. "I have an uncle who married a Frenchwoman. They live in the Bordeaux region of France, where her father's a winemaker. I've visited there since I was a kid, and my aunt has taught me a lot."

"The job's yours, then."

I laughed. "I said I know a *little*. I can't take the job, of course, but I could help you talk to candidates while I'm here."

"Really?" Brad lifted his drink in a toast. "That would be great. Thanks, man."

"Happy to help. Especially since you're looking into the Patty situation for me."

"I've got a folder full of résumés," Brad said. "I'd love it if you went through them and picked out the ones I should interview. Then, if you can stay awhile, you can sit in on the interviews with me."

"Sure."

"What about your work, Ennis?" Daphne asked.

"I'm between jobs right now. Not an issue."

I'd chosen to leave college, and I'd begun working at a marketing firm when I returned to London after Patty left. After the dream, I felt I urgently needed to come to the States, so I asked for time off. They said no, so I quit.

"If you're going to be around for a while," Daphne said, "you should stay here instead of the hotel. We have plenty of room. Right, Brad?"

Brad's facial muscles tensed, but only for a split second. "Yeah, sure. Love to have you."

Why would that bother him? He just asked for my help hiring a winemaker.

"All right," I said. "I appreciate it. I'll pack up in the morning and head back over here."

Brad and I took our drinks into his office, where he showed me his file full of winemaker résumés.

After about an hour, Daphne entered.

"Hey," she said. "You want me to have Cliff go to town and bring your stuff from the hotel? It's late. You may as well spend the night here."

"Cliff isn't supposed to leave you unguarded," Brad said.

She let out a soft scoff. "This place is like a vault. No one can get in."

"Your safety isn't up for debate." Brad rose. "I have to take care of a few things. You two stay in here as long as you'd like."

I waved to Brad. "I'll be fine," I said to Daphne. "If it gets too late, I'll just crash here and pick up my stuff tomorrow."

"Okay. Whatever you want." Daphne nodded to the folder. "Any good prospects?"

"A few. It's nice to have a project."

"Ennis..."

"Yeah?"

"What happened in London? With your job, I mean."

I paused a moment. Then, "Nothing. I quit."

"Why?"

"Simple. I asked for some time off to come here, and they said no."

"Why'd they say no?"

"Because I haven't worked there very long. They asked if it was an emergency, and I said no. I should have lied. Anyway, they said I couldn't have the time off, so I quit."

"Was that wise?"

"I didn't come here for judgment, love. I told you how freaky the dream was. I had to come."

She nodded. "I miss her too."

I hold up a hand. "Daph, this isn't about missing her. It's about finding the truth."

"If anyone can find the truth, Brad can."

"That's what I'm counting on," I said. "Besides, maybe I'll stay over here. Get myself one of those green-card jobbies and work here in the States."

"Won't you miss your home?"

"Of course. But I was ready to stay for four years to study. I only went home because Patty jilted me."

"And you came back because of Patty."

"I did. Which makes me think this is where I should be now."

"Do you think you'll go back to school?"

"I might. My student visa is still valid."

"What if we could find something for you to do around here? On the ranch?"

"I don't think I'm qualified to do anything here."

"Brad already offered you the job as winemaker."

"And I told him I wasn't qualified."

"But you're qualified to *choose* a winemaker?"

"More qualified than Brad is."

She nodded. "All right. Assistant winemaker, then. That'll be your job."

I laughed. "Are you allowed to go around offering jobs on the ranch?"

"Why not?" Daphne whipped her hands to her hips. "I'm mistress of the ranch, aren't I?"

"I'd love to stay here, but let's see what Brad has to say, okay?"

"All right. Wherever you end up, make sure it's somewhere

close. I've missed having a friend around."

"You got it." I shuffled the stack of papers. "These five look like they have the most promise. Where'd Brad go?"

"Out."

"Out where?"

"He didn't say."

"Does he go out this late a lot?"

"More often than I'd like for him to, but not every night, if that's what you mean."

"I'm sorry, love."

A few days later, I hired Bruce Gershwin as the first Steel winemaker.

Brianna

"I thought *you* were the first Steel winemaker," Donny said.

"No. Bruce was, but he was only there for a bit. I took over after he left, and I'm the one who trained Ryan."

"I've never heard his name before," Donny says. "Everyone always says you were the first winemaker."

"I wasn't."

Winemaker, winemaker. Who cares? "Okay...but how did my grandmother end up with the ring?" I press.

"I refused to leave Snow Creek until I had an answer about Patty," Ennis says.

Ennis

"Ennis will be working with you as your assistant," Brad said to Bruce. Then, to me, "Daphne tells me you're thinking about staying in the States."

"If I can get a green card."

"Consider it done," Brad said. "I'll have my attorneys handle it."

"This is a big step," I said.

"If you're going to turn me down, tell me now," Brad said. "That way, Bruce can bring in his own people."

"I don't have any people," Bruce said.

"Seems like kismet, then. What do you say, Ennis? You can both hire who you need."

I stood and held out my hand. "Deal, Brad. Thank you."

The next night, Daphne and I had dinner together at her house. Brad wasn't there—he rarely was—and Daphne's mother-in-law had excused herself early.

I got right to the point.

"Has Brad checked with the Peace Corps yet?" I asked Daphne. "About Patty?"

"Not that he's told me."

Damn. Was Patty a priority to Brad Steel at all? Was Daphne? His child? He was never home, and he basically gave the responsibility of his up-and-coming winery to me, an Englishman.

Daphne sighed. "Maybe it's time to let her go. Maybe we both need to let her go, Ennis."

Let her go?

The Australian diamond ring sat in the pocket of my jeans, and I absently touched it through the denim.

I couldn't let her go.

I just couldn't.

But perhaps Daphne was right.

I finally nodded. "You're right, love. I just didn't want to think our relationship meant nothing to her, and when I had that dream, I had a sliver of hope and a sliver of dread at the same time. I don't want her dead, of course, but part of me wants to believe I meant something to her."

"Of course you did."

"Perhaps. But the Peace Corps apparently meant more. Something she never even discussed with me." I threw my gaze to the floor. "It doesn't make any sense."

"It doesn't. But like I said, Patty isn't the first friend who's left me in the dust, never to be heard from again, which makes me think maybe it's not that abnormal of a thing."

Again I felt horrid for her at that thought.

Why should anyone think it's normal to lose people they love? Young people.

I pulled the ring out of my jeans pocket and stared at it.

Daphne's eyes went wide. "Oh my. You were going to propose to her, weren't you?"

"I'd hoped to. It was false hope. I knew she wasn't here. Even if the dream had turned out to be true, it wasn't a good dream, Daphne. She was hurt. Or dead. Or something." I rubbed my forehead. "It's so hard to even say the words. I suppose I hope she is in Africa. At least then she's all right." I fingered the platinum band and the large orange stone surrounded by clear diamonds. "This belonged to my great-grandmother from Australia. It's a fire diamond, and it's worth...well... a lot."

"I wish I could have seen it on Patty's finger," Daphne said. "It would have gone so perfectly with her hair."

"I know." A smile edged onto my lips. "I hated the thing when Mum gave it to me. Thought it was an awful color. Until I met Patty. I fell hard for her, and I knew then why Mum had given me the ring. It was for Patty."

"Maybe someday..." Daphne said wistfully.

But I shook my head adamantly. "No. I'm letting her go, Daph, which means I can't hold on to this."

"Sure you can. You'll meet someone else."

"I don't want to meet anyone else. How do you get over the love of your life?"

"I don't... I don't know."

"Tell me this. If something happened to Brad, would you get over him?"

She closed her eyes. "I can't let my mind go there."

"And that's what I mean." I grabbed her hand and shoved the ring into it. "It's for you, Daph. Keep it. Give it to one of your children. Maybe you'll have a girl next. Or wear it. Just keep it. I know you're going to have a huge family."

"Ennis, I can't. You don't know. You may want it back."

"All right. You keep it for me, then. I've got all the papers with me. I'll give them to you. Put it in a safe, and if I ever ask for it back, you'll have it."

She smiled then. "All right, Ennis. If that's what you want."

"It is."

But I knew I'd never ask for it back.

Brianna

"Such a sad story," Callie says. "You never wanted it back?"

"I never did. Then, when Daphne died—or so we thought— shortly after Marjorie was born, I never thought about the ring again."

"Turns out it was stolen from our mother," Donny says. "It was left for me in a safe-deposit box by a woman named Brittany Sheraton. We found out she and her father had been paid off in jewels for helping to run a human trafficking ring on some property of ours in Wyoming." He shakes his head. "It's a long story. A big mess. Anyway, one of their payments included the ring. We didn't know who it belonged to when I found it, but I always thought it would be perfect for Callie."

"Then Callie should have it," Ennis says.

"I couldn't," Callie says, gazing at her own engagement ring, the replica. "This one is beautiful, and I really think the ring should be with you, Ennis."

Ennis shakes his head. "What would I do with it? I never married. I have no offspring to leave it to. Please. It should be yours."

"Are you sure?" Donny asked.

Ennis smiles. "I can't believe how good I actually feel after finally telling that story after so many decades. I feel ten years younger. Truly. But still, I won't be on this earth a whole lot longer. I always thought the ring was meant for Patty, and if she'd lived, I know she'd still be wearing it and we'd have grandchildren to leave it to." He sighs. "But she didn't live. And I know now that she didn't leave me of her own accord. So the ring isn't hers. It never was. It was waiting to find its true owner." He takes Callie's hand, kisses the back of it. "And it has, my dear. Be a good wife to Donny, and Donny, you be a good husband to her. And I'll always know that Mum's ring is in good hands."

CHAPTER THIRTEEN

Jesse

My visit with Dragon at the hospital was short. He wasn't up for much more than a quick conversation. He was still exhausted and clearly somewhat embarrassed and ashamed by his circumstances.

Leaving him was not easy, but I had no choice.

Brock upgraded us all to first-class seating for the four-and-a-half-hour train ride to Edinburgh, and after the fiasco with the plane ride over here and losing my luggage, I didn't balk at it. I'm a slow learner, but I eventually learn.

Or I try to, anyway. It still sticks in my craw for sure, but at least I'm comfortable.

The seats are covered in red brocade and are comfortably plush. I sit with Brock and Rory, a table between our seats.

Dinner is served on the train, beginning with a smoked salmon roulade. I've never had it before. It's thinly sliced smoked salmon with cream cheese that's got some kind of herb in it, and it's drizzled with a vinaigrette.

Surprisingly, it's good. I eat most things, and I love fish. I've just never had it this way before.

Our soup—yes, we get a soup course on the train—is Cullen skink. Can't say I'm impressed with the name, but according to the menu, it's a traditional Scottish soup made with smoked haddock, potatoes, onions, and cream and seasoned with herbs and spices. Surprisingly good as well. Then again, I like fish.

Across the aisle from us, Maddie scrunches up her nose.

"Try it, Maddie," I say. "It's pretty good."

"It smells weird."

"That's the haddock," Brianna says. She's sitting next to my sister.

"I know..." She takes a bite. "All right, so it's not terrible, but I don't think I'm going to waste the calories. That salmon thing was good, though."

Brianna is sitting next to the window across the aisle from us, so I can't really see her. I'm alone in my row. Dragon would've been sitting with me.

Cage and Jake are sitting across from Maddie and Brianna.

Our main course comes—roast beef.

"Not as good as Steel beef," Brock says, of course.

"I don't think they get Steel beef in the UK, do they?" Rory asks.

"Our distribution system is pretty much domestic only," he says.

"I think it's good," I can't help saying.

It's not a lie at all. The beef is served—again, according to our printed menu—with a red wine reduction sauce and roasted potatoes, root vegetables, and a Yorkshire pudding, which of course I've never had before. It turns out to be something kind of like a popover. It's delicious, very savory. It tastes very...beefy.

"You like your Yorkshire pudding, Jess?" Rory says.

"Yeah. It's so good."

Dessert turns out to be sticky toffee pudding.

I rise after I finish my dessert.

My dick is already hardening, just being this close to Brianna.

Damn it all to hell.

"Excuse me," I say to Brock and Rory. "I'm going to hit the loo."

"Loo?" Rory raises her eyebrows with a chuckle.

"When in Rome," I say.

I walk through our coach to the end, where the bathrooms are located—one on each side. One is occupied, so I take the vacant one. I don't actually have to go the bathroom, but I unbuckle my belt anyway and release my cock.

I give it a few good pulls, but it's not working for me. Damn.

Just my luck. I can't even jack off with Brianna Steel here. She is all that will do it for me.

Which means...celibacy.

I rearrange my junk quickly, pull my pants back up, and wash my hands.

Then I open the door.

Brianna stands there.

I don't think.

I only feel.

And then I act.

I yank her arm, pulling her into the small bathroom.

"Jesse—"

I crush my mouth down on hers.

She opens for me instantly, and our tongues tangle. She tastes of the sticky toffee pudding, sugar, caramel.

My cock is raging now—raging to get inside Brianna's tight pussy.

This restroom is tiny, though not quite as tiny as one on an airplane.

I don't care. I reach for the door to lock it, never once breaking the passionate kiss.

I deepen the kiss, melting into her body, until—

She pushes me away, my back shoving into the counter where the sink is.

"Jesse, what are you—"

"You want this," I say, my breath coming in rapid puffs. "You want this as much as I do. Tell me you do."

"I... I don't know. I want you. Yes. But here—" Her dark gaze sears into my mind.

I crush my mouth onto hers again.

She doesn't push me away this time. Instead, she grinds into me. The counter digs into my back, but I don't care. All I care about is satisfying the craving for Brianna Steel.

Distractions...

No more distractions...

Except...

Something...

I need something to get me through this tour. To help me blow off the steam that gets pent up inside me. That threatens to drive me insane.

Focus.

I have to focus.

But a man *needs*...

A man needs...

She pulls back again, this time our mouths coming apart with a smack.

"Jesse... Not here..."

"Where then? Where, Brianna? You know I have nothing to offer you. Nothing. But damn..." I rake my fingers through my hair. "I can't be around you and not want you. Not need you."

She smiles then.

And *oh my God...*

There's a reason she wanted me to take her virginity. Something I've been blind to. Something I just didn't want to see, so I ignored it.

But my subconscious knows. Has always known.

"I..." Her voice quivers. "I love you, Jesse."

"Fuck," I growl.

What the hell is love, anyway? I've been in love before. And it didn't feel anything like this. This raw and visceral necessity for another person.

No matter how angry Brianna makes me—and manipulating me into taking her virginity made me mad as hell—I can't get her out of my mind.

Love?

No, this goes beyond love.

Love is sweet and nice and kind.

What I feel for Brianna Steel isn't nice at all. Not sweet. Not kind.

It's a raw and animalistic passion that I can't seem to control.

It's *need* more than love. Lust more than desire. Raw more than sweet.

What I feel for Brianna Steel isn't nice at all.

It's nasty.

Dark and nasty and full of hunger. It's an urge to take, a yearning to possess...

What the fuck has happened to me?

This is my big chance. Rory's big chance. The band's big chance.

And when I'm not focusing on my goals, what's best for the band and this tour... All I can think about is Brianna's silky brown hair, her doe-like dark eyes with lashes like a black curtain. Her gorgeous body—legs that go on forever. Tits as luscious as I've ever seen.

And that tight little cunt of hers—so snug that it fits me better than any other has.

I love you, Jesse.

I yearn to return the words. But are they true?

Is raw need the same as love?

"J-Jesse?" she says, her voice raspy.

I shake my head, meeting her dark gaze. God, those eyes, those lashes.

Those full pink lips that are trembling ever so slightly.

Those tits, so gorgeous in that Dragonlock T-shirt.

And her legs. Her legs covered in denim, her feet in cowboy boots.

My cowgirl.

My fucking cowgirl.

She's a rancher. Brianna's a rancher. She'll stay with her father in Colorado and work his ranch.

But she's not there now.

No. She's here. With me. On a train bound to Edinburgh.

She'll be with me for the next few months, traveling around Europe.

And I need...

I need...

I need *her.*

I fucking need *her.*

"Brianna..." I growl.

"Y-Yes?"

"I...need you. I want you. I have to have you."

She frowns. "But you don't love me."

"Damn it, Brianna, you don't love me either. You've built me up in your head for God knows how long. You love the *idea* of me."

"No." She gulps. "That's not true. I know exactly who you are, Jesse. And I love you. I've always loved you."

"But you don't know love, Bree. You can't. You're too—"

"Young?" she finishes for me. "Don't you dare tell me what I can and can't feel. I've known for a long time that you're my one and only. If you can't return my love, I can't force you to, but don't you dare tell me I'm not feeling what I know in my heart I'm feeling. I ache for you, Jesse. I've ached for you for so long. An eternity, it seems sometimes."

"Bree—"

"Stop it." She clamps her hand over my mouth. "Just stop it. What do you want to do, Jesse? Why did you drag me in here? To fuck me? If that's the case, do it. I won't stop you. I want it as much or more than you do."

"Don't say that to me unless you mean it."

"Haven't you figured out by now that I never say anything I don't mean?" She reaches forward in the small compartment and grabs my collar. "You need me. I want all of you, Jesse, but if you can't give me everything, I'll take what I can get. Just for the tour. Just for—"

I crush my mouth to hers again.

I'll take her. She's giving, and I will take.

It's not a fair exchange. I know this, but so does she.

And if she's offering?

I'd be a fool to say no.

CHAPTER FOURTEEN

Brianna

He rips his mouth from mine, turns me away from him, and then moves so I'm facing the counter. I brace myself in the small train bathroom as Jesse reaches around and unsnaps and unzips my jeans. He shoves them down over my hips, and then he grabs my ass underneath my lacy black thong.

"Fuck, Brianna..." he growls against my ear.

He squeezes my ass cheeks again before yanking the thong down.

Then the clink of his belt buckle, the zing of his zipper.

And his huge cock is inside me. It's a tight fit, as my legs aren't spread, and it burns into me like a sword of fire.

He goes balls deep, and he groans against me.

"Feel that, Brianna? Feel me inside you? How well I fit?"

"Yes," I gasp out.

He stays inside me, and though I long for the friction of his thrusts, I revel in the fullness. Completeness.

Until—

He pulls out, tickling my pussy lips with the head of his cock for a few seconds, and then he thrusts back into me.

God, the fullness once more. The completeness. Again he stays inside me. Completes me.

"I could fucking *live* inside you," he rasps against my neck.

"God, you feel so perfect."

If only...

If only he meant those words.

But he's speaking in the moment because it feels so good to him.

It feels so good to *me*.

Again he pulls out and plunges back into me.

Already I'm heading toward the peak. I need to touch my clit, but I can't while I'm bracing myself in this tiny area. My nipples are hard and aching.

So I close my eyes, imagine Jesse's talented tongue between my legs, sucking on my clit. I undulate my hips, meeting him thrust for thrust for thrust.

And—

"God, Jesse," I grit out in a whisper.

"Yeah, baby," he growls. "You come for me. Only for me. Just me. Because you're mine, Brianna. You're fucking *mine*."

He plunges in me, so deep that I swear I can feel him touch my heart and soul.

As I soar over the Highlands, I feel every pulse of his cock as he fills me.

He fills more than my pussy.

He fills my heart.

He fills my soul.

And I can't help myself.

"I love you, Jesse."

My words float in the enclosed space, and in my mind, I hear him return them.

I love you too, Brianna. I love you too.

But as my orgasm subsides, reality sinks in.

The words were from Jesse's mouth, in Jesse's voice...

But they were only in my mind.

I open my eyes, see my reflection in the mirror. My eyes are glassy, but I refuse to let the tears come. This is what I asked for. This is what I wanted, and I have no regrets.

He stays inside me for a few timeless moments, and when he pulls out, I hold back my whimper at the loss.

I turn around to face him, and he wipes me gently with a tissue. Then he pulls up his underwear and jeans, and I notice he's wearing the belt buckle I gave him. I quickly fasten my jeans and then reach out and trace the engraved dragon with my finger.

"You like it?" I ask.

"I love it."

A smile spreads across my face. "I'm glad. I knew it was yours the moment I saw it."

"Brianna..."

I touch my fingers to his lips. "You don't have to say anything. First of all, I didn't intend to have my name on the engraving. The clerk made a mistake, and then he gift wrapped it in that gorgeous red dragon paper. I should have unwrapped it to make sure the engraving was right."

"If you had, would you have still given it to me?"

His question is valid, and I have to think about it. Would I have?

"Probably not," I tell him. "You weren't supposed to know it was from me."

"Bree..."

"Yeah?"

He draws in a breath, holding it for a few seconds. "How long have you...felt this way about me?"

My cheeks warm. Then they tingle, as if I can feel the

blood rushing to them and making them pink. "Seems like forever."

"You deserve someone who can love you back."

"I know."

"So..."

"You're the one I want, Jesse. If I can't have you long term, I'll take what I can get."

He shakes his head. "That's crazy, Bree. I mean...I'm a man. I want you desperately, and I want to take you up on what you're offering. But I'm not a user. I don't use women, and I'm not about to start now."

"You won't be using me."

"Please..."

He's right, of course. "Look at it this way, then. We'll be using each other. You can't give me what I ultimately want. I can accept that. But I want as much of you as I can get, so I'll take what you're offering."

And maybe, I add to myself, you'll fall in love with me during this tour. Maybe you'll find out we're meant to be.

But this isn't a fairy tale. I'm not Cinderella, and Jesse isn't Prince Charming, searching all over for the woman who fits only my shoe.

I draw in a breath, look him straight in his gorgeous brown eyes.

"Brianna, I'm not going to fall in love with you."

"I understand, Jesse. You don't have to beat me over the head with it." I turn back to the sink and wash my hands.

He touches my shoulder, and I look up to see his reflection in the mirror.

His brown eyes are haunted—almost beautifully haunted.

"I don't have the right to ask you for this," he says, "but

I need you, Brianna. I need to focus on this tour, but I also need to be able to let go. You give me that. I can't promise you anything beyond this tour, and I have no right to ask any of this of you, but—"

My heart cracks a little, but at least he's being honest with me.

He's not lying to get into my pants, like a lot of men would do.

"Whatever you need, Jesse," I say. "I want this tour to be a success. I wish I could have fixed everything with Dragon."

"What?" He turns me around and meets my gaze. "What happened with Dragon wasn't your problem to fix."

"I just... I want..."

He pulls me into an embrace. "You're such a wonderful woman, Brianna."

"You're a wonderful man," I reply.

He lets go of me. "You want to go out first?"

"Sure. But you've been gone longer."

"If anyone asks, I'll say the meal didn't agree with me. Okay?"

I nod, touch his cheek with a sad smile, and then I leave the bathroom.

CHAPTER FIFTEEN

Jesse

If anyone wondered why I took so long in the bathroom, they don't mention it, thank God. We arrive in Edinburgh and check in at the Waldorf Astoria.

The fucking Waldorf Astoria, courtesy of Brock.

For once, I don't complain. Instead, I force my appreciation out. "Thank you, Brock. This is very generous of you."

Brock's eyebrows fly upward. Of course he's surprised. I'm usually a dick about this stuff.

"You're welcome," Brock says. "Rory and I thought it best if we stay where Emerald Phoenix is staying, same as London."

I nod. "Yes, that's a good idea."

And something inside me floats away, like a lump of coal that was lodged in my gut but is now gone.

Brock is Rory's fiancé, and Donny is Callie's fiancé. They're in love with my sisters, and they want to help.

Instead of whining about it, I should allow it. For the good of the band.

Instead of feeling ashamed that I can't offer the band these kinds of accommodations, I should be grateful that Brock is here and is willing.

And I am.

I'm fucking grateful.

Taking what's offered doesn't make me weak. It doesn't make me not good enough.

It's taking a gift and giving back when I can.

I'll repay Brock and Donny someday. Somehow. But for now? I will take what they offer for the good of the band. And I'll try not to feel shitty about it.

Taking isn't bad.

Except when it is.

I took from Brianna, and she will allow me to continue to take.

I should be strong enough to resist her.

I should be a lot of things.

But I've told her where I stand, and she still wants to be with me. I don't want to be a dick. I don't want to lead her on.

I only want what's best for her.

What's best for the band.

What's best for the band is for me to be focused, and the only way I can be focused is if Brianna is out of my head.

And the only way for her to be out of my head is for me to take what she's offering.

My room is nice with two queen beds. It was originally meant for Dragon and me, but since he isn't here...

Brianna is rooming with Maddie, of course. I won't see her tonight. We've already had dinner, and we all need a good night's rest because tomorrow evening is the Edinburgh concert.

I grab my phone and dial Callie.

"Hey, Jess," she says.

"Hey. We're here safely, and I wanted to check in on you guys and Dragon."

"He's good. He was discharged a few hours ago, and we're back at the hotel. Donny will be staying with him in his room."

"Thanks for that. I didn't want to ask, but..."

"It's not a problem, Jesse. We want him to get well as much as you do. And he does, too. He feels terrible about everything."

"Is he there? Can I talk to him?"

"Yup. He's right here. We're in his room. Donny's getting his things moved. Here he is."

"Jess," Dragon says.

"Dragon, man. How are you?"

His sigh whooshes through the phone and into my ear. "I feel like the world's biggest asshole, man. I swear to God, Jess. I didn't take anything. Those bitches must have slipped me something."

"But you don't remember..."

"I know I don't. But I swear. I never would have."

I hear truth in his words. He's not lying. Not to me. Not when he knows what's at stake. What he almost fucked up.

"I believe you, buddy."

"I know. And you know I'd never lie to you."

"I know you wouldn't. Do you need rehab?"

"I'll be okay. I'll force it. I want to join the rest of you guys in Paris. I swear to God, I'll make it happen."

"You doing okay?"

"Detox is a bitch, but I've been through worse. There was fentanyl in my system, but I'm on methadone for a few days to help get me back to normal. I refused it at first, but then I figured why not take all the help I can get? I can do it, Jess. I've walked through fire and survived. I can do this."

I believe him. I believe him with all my heart. Because in truth? This is nothing compared to other stuff Dragon has been through.

"Yeah, you can, man. I'm in your corner. Always."

"I know you are, Jesse. I'm just so sorry I ever started talking to those women. You had the right idea to get the fuck out of there."

Yeah, I did. But only because I had eyes only for Brianna. If not for Brianna? It could have been me in there with Dragon getting drugged.

Fuck.

Maybe I owe Brianna for this one.

Cage and I had decided to fuck our way across Europe. And if not for my aching desire for Brianna Steel, I'd have been with Dragon and...

God, I can't go there.

We were able to replace a drummer, but they couldn't have replaced me.

Brianna...

God...I've been blaming her for distracting me.

But if she hadn't...

Fuck...

I owe her everything.

I text her quickly.

You still up?

Yeah.

Can you come to my room?

It's almost nine o'clock, Jesse. I'm exhausted from the train ride.

I know. But I have to talk to you. It's
important.

The three dots linger for longer than makes me comfortable, until—

Be right there.

I text her my room number quickly and then head to the bathroom and check myself out in the mirror. I look like I've been traveling all day, which I have. Not all day, perhaps, but for the last five hours.

I wash my hands and face and eye the plush white robe that's hanging in the bathroom.

It would be so much more comfortable...

But no. This isn't a booty call. I want to tell her thank you.

I want to tell her...

God, so much I'd like to tell her.

So much I can never say to her.

Because I'm not sure what I'm feeling.

It's new to me...

Foreign...

Something I've...

Oh my God.

Something I've never felt before. Something stronger than the love I've known. Something more physical and visceral. Yet it's far from only physical and visceral.

And it may...

It may be that silly four-letter word that Brianna utters so freely.

But I can't.

I won't.

Because if I do, I'll mean it.

I'll mean it with all my heart.

She believes she means it. But she's young, and worshipping someone from afar for years isn't love. It's infatuation. Lust. Puppy love, even.

Not the all-encompassing passion and desire and pure urge to protect that I'm feeling now.

Fuck. It. All.

I may truly be in love with Brianna Steel, even after I assured her I wasn't and could never be.

And then...

A knock on my door.

CHAPTER SIXTEEN

Brianna

Jesse opens the door and looks amazing as always. He's still wearing the black button-down and jeans, complete with leather belt and the dragon belt buckle that he wore on the train.

I've showered, and my hair is damp and hanging around my shoulders. No makeup, and I had just pulled on a pair of lounge pants and a Dragonlock tank when he called. My feet are bare, even in February.

He holds the door open, and I enter. On the table are two glasses of water. He motions to one. "Thirsty?"

I nod, walk over, and pick up a glass. "I don't know what it is about traveling, but it's very dehydrating."

Or maybe it was the fuck in the bathroom. I can't say I've joined the mile-high club, but a train bathroom has to mean something. I take a drink, letting it soothe my dry throat.

He picks up the other glass and drains it. Then he looks at me but says nothing.

I clear my throat. "Since you called me here, I kind of thought you'd start."

He nods. "Yeah. I... I want to thank you."

I raise my eyebrows. "For what? The fuck? You don't have to thank me for that. I don't do anything I don't want to."

"For Christ's sake, Bree. No, not for the fuck." He inhales deeply and gazes at me. "Though that was crazy hot."

I smile. "It was."

He rakes his fingers through his unruly hair and tugs on it. "I talked to Dragon."

"How's he doing?"

"He's going to be fine, and he swears he didn't take anything. He's pretty sure he was drugged."

"Yeah. That's so awful. But I'm glad he's going to be okay."

"The thing is, Bree..."

I smile. "You're calling me Bree."

"That's your name, isn't it?"

"You usually call me Brianna." Is that even true, though? He's called me Bree before. I'm trying to find something new and different, hoping for what he already told me in no uncertain terms would never happen.

"Brianna, then."

"No. Call me Bree. I like it." I move toward him, my body already responding to him.

"For God's sake." He inhales, holding up a hand to keep me away from him. "This isn't a booty call. I just want you to know that."

"I wouldn't mind if it was."

"Oh my God." He paces back toward the table, refills his water from the pitcher, and drains it again. He heads back to me. "Just listen, will you? I want to thank you, and not for the fuck."

I open my mouth to speak, but he gestures me to keep quiet.

"Please. Just let me finish."

I nod. "Okay."

He gestures to his bed. "Sit."

I obey.

How easy it is to obey Jesse Pike.

The room has two queen beds, and the bed is firm. Better than mine in the room I'm sharing with Maddie. In fact, this is a much nicer room. It's bigger, and the fixtures are classier. Not that mine aren't classy. This *is* the Waldorf Astoria.

"Listen. Just listen, please. I want to thank you because... because of what happened to Dragon. It could have easily happened to me."

I swallow. Jesse? Drugged and in a hospital right now? I can't even let myself think of it. "What exactly are you saying?" I ask him.

"Dragon had four women. *Four*, Brianna."

I guess he's done with Bree. And I don't like where this conversation is heading. I'm not sure what to say, so I settle on, "Okay..."

"Four," he repeats. "They wanted both of us, and he had arranged to bring them back to the hotel in our limo. I realized I didn't want that, and when I left, two of the women left as well. I left the other two in the room with Dragon. Big mistake. Except it turns out it wasn't a mistake."

"You met Maddie and me with Zane."

He rubs his hand over his forehead. "God, that's another whole story, but yeah. I'm glad I nipped that in the bud."

I draw in a breath. He's being honest with me, so I may as well be honest with him. "I was determined to do it. I didn't like the idea, but I thought it might help get my mind off you."

"God. I'm sorry I reduced you to that. And I'm damned glad I intervened. Not just for Maddie, but for you too."

My lips edge up into a smile.

"But that's not why I'm thanking you either. If you hadn't been on my mind..." He buries his face in his hands. "Shit, this is hard for me."

I rise and close the distance between us. I move his hands from his face and cup his stubbled cheek. "Just say it, Jesse. Say what you want to say to me."

"If I hadn't had you on my mind, I'd have stayed with Dragon and the women, and I would probably have been drugged as well."

I scrape my fingers over his jawline. "But you didn't. And you weren't drugged."

"And it's a damned good thing I wasn't. We were able to replace a drummer."

"But no one could have replaced you," I say, the truth finally dawning on me. "That's why you're thanking me."

"Yeah. Because of you, I wasn't there. I was..."

"With me."

"Yeah. And I've been punishing myself for not being there for Dragon, when the truth is, if I *had* been there, I'd have fucked everything up beyond repair."

"Oh, Jesse..."

He grips my shoulders, almost shaking me. "You're inside me, Brianna. Inside me like a fucking sickness. It's driving me insane. I didn't plan this, and I don't want to lead you on."

A sickness? Insanity? Hardly words of love and affection, but the look on Jesse's face tells another story. He feels something—something he doesn't want to feel.

Brianna, I'm not going to fall in love with you.

The words he uttered mere hours ago on the train. In the bathroom, after we fucked. I pause a moment. Gather my thoughts. Try to put my feelings in the back of my mind.

"We already talked about this, Jesse. I'll be with you during the tour. I'll help you keep your focus."

"I don't like to use women."

"You're not using me. Again, at the risk of repeating myself, we've been through this. You're not using me if I know the deal and I'm good with it anyway."

"Fuck." He pulls me to him and kisses me hard.

I've grown to know how he kisses—how he pries my lips apart with his tongue and then he plunges it inside my mouth. How his lips slide against mine, how our teeth clash together because it's always a breathless and needy kiss.

He breaks it almost as quickly.

"God, how I wish..." he says on a sigh.

"You wish what?"

"I wish... I wish I knew what you truly felt. What you're truly after... How you..."

Then he crushes his lips to mine again.

We groan into each other's mouths, and he slides one hand over my chest and cups my breast, thumbing my nipple through my tank top.

He breaks the kiss again. "Do you know how much it turns me on when you wear Dragonlock stuff? I mean, I've seen it on a lot of women, and it never did to me what you wearing it does to me."

I sigh against him. "Jesse..."

"Damn it, Brianna. I wasn't looking for this. I'm not ready for this, and you're..." He caresses my face, moves a piece of damp hair out of my eyes. "You're not..."

Again the kiss. Our lips meet in a clashing thunder of sparks and deafening chorus.

Cymbals crash together, and the brass sections rumble

around the percussion.

No flutes and clarinets for Jesse and me. No oboe or strains of a violin or cello.

No. Only brass and percussion—the sounds of lust and desire and electrically charged passion.

He walks forward, backing me toward the bed I was just sitting on.

Then he breaks the kiss and inhales sharply. "I didn't mean for this to be a booty call."

"I know that. But if you need it, it's okay with me."

"No." He steps away from me, rubbing his forehead. "That's not what I mean."

"What exactly do you mean, Jesse?" I gesture toward him, beckoning him to me. "I'm right here. I want you and you want me. I already gave you permission to—"

"Damn it, Bree! I don't want your permission. I want your..."

I walk toward him, and he's... He's shaking. A slight tremble as he turns away from me.

"What *do* you want?" I ask softly.

He turns and meets my gaze, and I swear his brown eyes have darkened to coal black. "I want what you can't give me."

"What more can I give? I've given you everything. Even my heart, but you don't want that."

He grabs me then, his hold so forceful it actually hurts my upper arms. But I don't care. He's full of vim and vigor and fire and passion, and I love seeing him like this. It's the same vibe I get when he's onstage, singing.

He's got it for *me* now.

"You think you're giving me your heart, Bree. But what do you know of love?"

I absently place my hand on my chest, right over my heart. "I know what I feel."

"You know you've had a crush on a man for years. A man you didn't even know well until now. So much about me you *still* don't know, Brianna."

"I know all I need to know."

"If only it were that simple..." He shakes his head and releases me.

I stumble, and he grabs me to steady me. He looks at the red marks his fingers left on my arms. "I'm sorry. I didn't mean to hurt you."

"I know that."

"Physically, I mean. I'm afraid I've already hurt you emotionally."

"I'm a big girl." I brush my hands over my arms, easing the chill that has erupted. "I can handle this thing between us for the duration of the tour. I want it."

"I want it too. But it's not *all* I want."

Haven't I already told him I'd do whatever he needs? Whatever he wants? What more could he want? Does he want to handcuff me to the bed? Bind me? Spank me? I'll do it. I'll do it all for him.

"What, then? What do you need, Jesse? Because I'll move heaven and earth to get it for you."

He simply stares at me then. Doesn't try to get rough with me. Says nothing about changing the way we have sex. Nothing about tying me up or spanking me, even though the thought arouses me more than I thought it would.

"I will," I say again. "I'll move heaven and earth. I wanted so badly to be the one to fix the Dragon situation. I even asked Brock to fill in. He used to be a drummer in a garage band. I was going to scour the streets of London to find you a drummer. I wish I could have fixed it because I felt like it was my fault."

"No. Not your fault. Never your fault."

"I wish I could have fixed it," I repeat, "but I'm glad Jett and Heather could fix it for you because I never intended to interfere with your big chance. I was ready to leave. To go home. But I couldn't. Not after I promised Maddie that I'd do this trip with her. I couldn't go back on my word."

"No. And I wouldn't want you to." He stalks back toward me. "I want you here, Bree. I need you here."

"I'm not going anywhere." I grab his arms, caress his muscles that are so tense and tight. "So tell me what you want, Jesse. I gave you my heart. What else do you want?"

"Oh, Brianna..." He touches my cheek with such a gentle caress that I widen my eyes to make sure it's him and not a dove's wing.

Jesse's not known for his light touch.

"I *do* want your heart, Bree. But I'm not sure you've actually given it to me."

I drop my mouth open.

He gently pushes my chin upward so my mouth closes. "I can't believe this, but...I'm in love. I love you, Brianna. I didn't want to. I *don't* want to. But I do. And it crept up on me so quickly that I almost missed it. But it's fucking love. It's not the pretty and romantic kind of love that you want, though. It's the all-encompassing viral kind of love that will eat at your very soul. The kind of love that you know is true and pure because every love that came before it pales in comparison. The kind of forever love that's so genuine it fucking hurts, Bree."

The words...

Are they real?

Because he's told me time and again that there's no future. That he'll never love me. But Jesse wouldn't lie to me. Not about something so important.

Still, I'm afraid to hope...

"You *love* me?" I say, my lips quivering.

"God, yes. I tried to fight it, but you're inside me, Bree. You're part of me now, and I'm not sure I can let you go if I give in to this."

I swallow. A big part of me is still afraid to believe his words. "Jesse, I don't want you to let me go."

"But... I know you *think* you love me. But you're young. This is a first love. And I'm telling you I was convinced I was in love when I was your age too, but this... *This*... This is so much more. It's like when the melody builds, and the harmony comes in, and it's perfect and comes to a fever pitch... It's the perfect blend... The perfect sound..."

I step back.

The look on his face is pure anguish. He's wincing, his eyes are glassy, his jaw rigid, and the wrinkles on his forehead are furrowed with tension. He's in pain. Jesse's in pain.

That's not how you should look after you tell a woman you're in love with her.

I swallow. "Why do you think I wouldn't return that kind of love?"

"Because it's too much for a kid like you."

Tension builds in my shoulders. He's not trying to make me angry. I know this, but again I have to remind him of the facts. "I'm twenty-two."

"I fucking *know* that, Bree. Twenty-two. First love. I'm concerned that what you feel for me is a crush, Brianna. And what I feel for you is so much more than that."

CHAPTER SEVENTEEN

Jesse

I can't believe I just said those words to her.

She looks at me with such passion, such desire. And it's all laced with a touch of anger.

Can I blame her? I basically just told her she's too immature to have real feelings for me. I'm lucky she hasn't slapped me.

"Jesse," she says, taking a step toward me, "that's all I ever wanted."

"No. I mean, maybe. How can I say this without being insulting? Because I'd rather die than insult you or make you feel bad in any way. But what you don't understand, Brianna, is the anguish I'm feeling inside me. *You're* inside me. You're a part of me now, and I want to fight it. I want to fight it so hard, and I've been trying to. But it doesn't work. Nothing works anymore, Bree. Because everything is you and everything is me."

She comes forward another step. "I can give you what you want, Jesse. I know I can."

I shake my head. Then I nod. "Maybe you can. I don't know. But I have to have you through this tour. Because releasing with you, letting my emotions out with you—it keeps me sane for the work I have to do."

She reaches toward me. "It's okay. I can give you what you need."

I know she thinks she can, but I'm done talking now. I grab her hand before she touches me, squeeze her wrist.

All I can think about is her, the need, the ache that I have for her, how part of me would give up this entire tour to be with her. I've been fighting it. Tamping it down.

And I can't tamp it down anymore.

The last forty-eight hours have been harrowing. First Dragon, and then finding a new drummer, and despite everything, it all worked out.

And while I was happy about that, something was missing.

What was missing was the woman standing before me now.

How did I let this happen?

How did I let this beautiful young woman not only into my heart, but into my very soul?

How did she become the essence of all that I am?

It's crazy, really. So crazy. But I need her, and I need her *now*.

I pull her to me and kiss her hard. I don't have to pry her lips open because she opens for me instantly, as if on instinct, as if the two of us are somehow fated to be together.

I slide my tongue over her teeth, her gums, the sides of her mouth, twirl it with her tongue, its velvety texture driving me slowly senseless.

She tastes of the remnants of bourbon.

She tastes of passion and desire and need and ache and want.

Her fingers gravitate to the collar of my shirt, and she begins to unbutton.

I grip the sides of her Dragonlock tank top and pull it up, exposing her breasts clad in a lacy bra. Still kissing her, I cup them, thumb her nipples through the lace.

She gasps into my mouth.

Then I pull back, breaking the suction of our mouths with a loud smack. The first two buttons of my shirt are undone, and I grab the two sides of it, rip them apart, letting the buttons fly and ping throughout the room.

My shirt is off, and I don't want to wait any longer. I quickly remove my shoes and socks, and then I unclasp the beautiful brass belt buckle. My gift from Brianna—Brianna, the woman I love.

I let my fingers graze the etching of the dragon, the letters of my name. Then I unclasp it, unsnap and unzip my jeans, push them over my hips along with my boxer briefs.

My cock juts out.

It's hard and aching, and I grasp it at the base, giving it a few quick pulls to try to ease my desire.

I want a night of lovemaking like we've never had.

I want to worship her body.

I want to ease the madness inside me.

"Brianna..." I growl.

"Yes, Jesse?" Her voice is a whisper full of lust and passion.

"Take off your clothes. Strip for me."

I've never asked a woman to strip for me before. Will she do it?

Her tank top is already sitting above her breasts. She doesn't smile. To the contrary, the look on her face is one of smoldering heat with narrowed eyes, slightly trembling lips— lips that are full and swollen from our passionate kiss.

Her tank top ends up on the floor, and then she unclasps

her bra from the back, shimmying out of it and letting her breasts fall gently against her chest. Her nipples are hard and erect, so beautiful with their brownish-red color.

Before she even starts on her jeans and cowboy boots, I reach toward her, grab both of her breasts and squeeze. They fill my palms with their gorgeous rosy flush, sitting in my hands like plump melons.

I graze my thumb over her nipples, relish her soft sigh, like a whisper on the wind.

And I hear lyrics in my head...

Her sigh like a whisper on the wind...

"God, your tits are beautiful, Brianna. They're works of art. I could write a song about their rosiness, their plumpness, those hard little nipples..." I pinch one, and then the other.

She gasps, closing her eyes.

"No. Watch me. I'm going to suck your nipples, Brianna. I'm going to pinch and twist one while I suck the other between my lips. And I want you to watch me do it. I want you to tell me how it feels. Pretend you're writing a song about it. Tell me exactly how I'm making you feel."

I lean down, take a nipple between my lips. I lick it gently at first, and then I suck it, loving the soft texture of it beneath my tongue.

I twist the other between my fingers, lightly at first, and then not so lightly.

"God, Jesse. You make me feel so good."

I let the nipple drop from my lips. "You like that?" I meet her gaze. "You like when I suck your pretty little nipples?"

"My God, Jesse, yes."

"Tell me, then. Tell me what I'm doing to you. Tell me what you feel inside your body when I suck those pretty nipples,

Brianna. Tell me where you feel it."

"My God... I feel it everywhere. I feel it in my nipples. In my breasts. Between my legs..."

"How does it feel between your legs, baby?"

"Like I need you. Like such an emptiness that I ache. Like I want to touch myself. But I'd rather have *you* touch me, Jesse. I'd rather have you lick me down there. Lick me so hard, and then stick your cock inside me."

My cock aches at her words.

Only now have I let myself feel what I truly feel.

And it occurs to me...

I've been feeling this way the whole time.

I would never have taken Brianna Steel to my bed if I wasn't feeling something amazing.

And it has nothing to do with the fact that her brother took my sister, or that her cousin took my other sister.

No, this is far from payback.

This is....

Love.

Love that I've never experienced before.

Love that I fear she won't be able to return because of her youth.

But I have to try.

I have to try to make it work.

I pull back from her. "Take off the rest of your clothes," I growl.

Her eyes are heavy-lidded now, and a beautiful pink flush graces her cheeks.

She takes a seat on the bed, pulls off her cowboy boots, and then rises, unsnapping and unzipping her jeans.

She slides them over her hips, along with a thong—this

one bright red.

I suck in a breath.

Her beautifully shaved pussy comes into view, and I can see that her lips are already swollen and glistening.

I grab her, sweep her into my arms, and lay her down on the bed, spreading her legs.

And then I gaze at the treasures between them.

I close my eyes and inhale her tangy scent.

Musk of Brianna.

Musk laced with tart apples and a tiny tinge of citrus.

I open my eyes, raise my head a bit, and meet her gaze. "I'm going to eat you, baby. I'm going to suck you and finger you and make you come so hard."

She sighs, leaning her head back, her hips rising.

I gaze at her a little longer, taking in the sheer beauty before me. I slide my tongue along her inner thighs, licking up the juices. She tastes like heaven. Heaven with a dash of sugar and spice.

"Please, Jesse..."

At her words, I slide my tongue over her slick folds, ending at her clit.

Her groans and words spur me on. I slide my tongue between her pussy lips into her heat. Then I move upward to her clit, swirling around it before sucking it gently between my lips.

"God, you taste good, baby."

I continue my assault on the treasures between her legs. Sliding from her pussy up to her clit, bringing her almost to the brink, and then sliding my tongue into her heat once more.

My cock is raging. So ready to plunge deep inside her pussy.

But I hold myself in check, giving it a few pulls to ease the ache. It doesn't help.

But I'm determined. Determined to make her come hard multiple times before I ease my own desire.

I spread her legs farther and then push her thighs forward, bringing her ass into my view. I slide my tongue over the puckered hole.

She gasps.

I stop.

Then I try again.

This time no gasp, so I continue. When her asshole is lubed up nicely, I slide my finger over it, careful not to breach. I massage it lightly.

And then a sigh from her beautiful lips.

Yes, she approves. Who wouldn't approve of a gentle ass massage?

How I long to stick my finger into the tight warmth. Breach that tight rim and show her what pleasures can be had at the back door.

But that's for another time.

I slide my tongue from her sweet asshole over her thighs where I kiss and nip the soft flesh. Then I head back to her clit, teasing it gently with my tongue, until I suck it between my lips and tug while simultaneously shoving two fingers into her pussy.

She grasps fistfuls of the comforter and arches her back as the orgasm pulses through her.

The walls of her pussy clench around my fingers, and I massage the anterior, focusing on her spongy G-spot.

Her name falls from my lips in harmony with the groans from my own.

It's a symphony around us. Her climax sings to me in notes I've never heard before.

"You come for me," I demand. "Sing for me."

I pull my fingers out of her pussy, slide my tongue over them, tasting her beautiful juices. Then I shove my fingers back into her heat, and with my thumb, I massage her clit.

She leaps again, and this time, the contractions of her pussy are even stronger.

God, what I wouldn't give to feel them around my cock.

But all in good time.

I continue my assault on her pussy as she comes down from her climax. I want to give her more. I want to give her a hundred more orgasms.

But my dick is ready.

I've got to satisfy myself, and then...

Then, I will kiss every part of this woman.

I'll make love to her body, to her heart and, I hope, to her soul.

"My God, Jesse... I don't think I've ever felt that way before."

I crawl toward her on the bed.

"I want to give you ten more orgasms just like that."

"I'm not sure I could take it. That one was... It was like something exploded in my brain. I didn't just feel it in my pussy. I felt it...everywhere. It was almost like I was out of my body and just floating in a sea of pure bliss."

Her words take me to the brink of insanity, and without answering, I climb on top of her and thrust my cock inside her.

She gasps, but she lifts her hips to meet me, and I thrust, thrust, thrust...

I don't want to come yet, so I pull out, move my hips

upward, and dangle my cock between her lips.

She closes them around it eagerly, sucking on the cock head.

"Yeah, baby. Lick your juices off my cock. Fuck, you're so hot."

I close my eyes, revel in her sweet lips around me. Love...

It's not what I thought it was.

At least not for me.

It's not sweet and gentle.

It's ferocious and aching and raw.

And the sex...

So different when this depth of emotion is involved.

And damn...

I fucking knew it all the time. The first time I shoved my cock into Brianna Steel's cunt, I felt something novel. Something I've never felt before. And it wasn't just her tight little body, her beautiful face, her infatuation with me.

No.

I found something I never knew I needed.

It's a fucking passion so intense and so much more than I've ever experienced with any other woman.

I told myself it was just physical chemistry.

But I knew for sure it wasn't when I saw her with Zane Michaels. With Maddie, it was pure protective instinct.

With Brianna? It was far more than that.

He was not going to touch what was mine.

And Brianna Steel is *mine*.

CHAPTER EIGHTEEN

B r i a n n a

I'm lost.

Lost in a sea of haze and bliss and perfect harmony.

Jesse...

Jesse loves me.

I'm living my dream.

My mouth is full of his cock, and I couldn't be happier, more excited, more enthralled.

Jesse Pike loves me.

I meet the rhythm of his cock, sucking him as he pulls it in and out of my mouth. He's huge, and blowing him isn't easy, but doing it gives me such unfettered joy.

If only I could stay in Jesse's room for the remainder of the tour.

But we must both think of Maddie.

He moves his cock from my mouth then, slides down my body, and kisses me hard. In another flash, his cock is inside me again.

And he's thrusting, thrusting, thrusting...

He rips his mouth away from mine. "I want to last longer," he grinds out, "but can't... Can't... Damn!"

He releases into me, and I take him in, not just with my pussy, but with my whole body and my whole heart.

He stays inside me for a few moments, and I relish the completeness. The pure joy and bliss of our joining.

When he pulls out and rolls over on his side, I snuggle into his arms. "You've made my dreams come true, Jesse," I say softly into his ear.

"This was never my dream," he says.

A wave of sadness slides through me. But then he kisses the top of my head.

"I mean that I didn't want this to happen," he continues. "But now that it has, I have to have you, Brianna. I'll give you all the time you need."

"I don't need any time, Jesse. I know what I feel. I've always known."

"You don't know what I'm asking of you," he says, his voice going dark.

"You're asking for my love. You *have* that."

"Yes. But I'm not *just* asking for your love. If we stay together, and if this band makes it big, where does that leave you?"

And in that second, with those words, he stabs a dagger into my heart.

Because my home is the ranch.

My home is working with my father. It's always been my dream, for longer than I've been in love with Jesse Pike.

But I don't need to think about that now. We don't know if Dragonlock is going to take off. This whole tour could lead to nothing.

But already I hear the lie in my own head.

After just two concerts, the band has broken even on their merchandise and made a bit of a profit.

Standing ovations at both concerts as well, even after they

lost their drummer.

Dragonlock is going places. There will be more tours, and eventually they will headline.

And if I stay with Jesse, that will mean...

No more Steel Ranch.

And as much as I love Jesse Pike, leaving the ranch will break my heart.

But I don't need to think about that right now.

Jesse loves me.

And somewhere, in the back of my mind, I always had doubts that my dream would come true.

Now that it's here, I've failed to consider everything it might mean. I'll have to make it work somehow.

At the moment, I can't be with him full-time anyway, as I've made so many promises to Maddie.

Maddie... And my brother...

"Jesse?"

"Yeah, baby?"

"What will we do for the rest of the tour? I mean, will we tell people? About us?"

He doesn't reply right away, and my nerves skitter across my flesh. Is he rethinking his feelings for me?

I berate myself for the thought. Jesse is a good man. An honest man. A proud man. A man who wouldn't say something to a woman that he didn't mean.

No. Jesse's feelings are real. And his fear is that mine are not. That they're just the lovesick musings of a young girl with a crush.

Even though I know they're not. My feelings are as real as his, and I've had them for so much longer.

"I honestly don't know," he finally says.

"I never told Maddie—or my cousins—how I felt about you. But I should probably tell you that Maddie asked me straight out if I had feelings for you."

"You mean before we went on the tour?"

"Yes. When I was trying to talk her into coming, you know, trying to talk her out of going back to school for her last semester."

"I get the feeling, Brianna, that your wanting Maddie along on this tour was not completely altruistic."

He's not wrong. And if he truly loves me, and because I truly love him, I must confess.

"Yes," I say. "I'm not proud of it, but that was the initial reason why I wanted Maddie to come along. But it didn't stay that way, Jesse."

"Oh?" His voice is tight.

He has the right to be pissed at my initial reasoning for wanting Maddie to come along. But I no longer feel that way, and I need to make that clear.

"No. I had no idea Maddie felt so left out of the little group with my cousins and me. We've always tried to include her. Please believe that."

He caresses my shoulder with his lips. "I believe that. Family is family. Family always trumps friends."

"So you *do* get it."

"Of course I get it, Brianna. Everything I do is for my family. This concert is for my family."

"I know that. And I'm going to try to never to forget it again."

He sighs. "That's the thing about you, Bree. And it's part of why I fought so hard against you. Not just your youth but your privilege. There are things about my family that you'll never understand."

"Donny and Brock understand."

"But do they? Perhaps Donny understands better than Brock. After all, Donny wasn't born into riches, and he remembers what his previous life was like."

A brick hits my stomach. Unless Callie told Jesse, he has no idea what Donny's previous life was really like. At least the last several months of it. It was way worse than anything any of the Pikes could have possibly been through.

I'm silent for a few moments, until, "I won't fault you that statement, Jesse. I do come from incredible privilege, and I know that. And yes, money is never a worry I've had. But I love you, and your worries are now my worries. Let me help you."

"See?" He exhales sharply. "This is why I fought these feelings, Brianna. As much as I want you, want to be with you, now is just not the optimal time. The band is taking off. This is my dream. Just like your dream is to work on the ranch alongside your father. My dream is only beginning. It's to make a living as a rock and roll singer. It's to be one of the great ones like Jett Draconis. It's to make my own living, take care of my family doing what I love to do and doing it well. My dream has never been to take money from someone else—even someone I love as much as I love you."

He still feels I'm immature. And in some ways, he's very right. So I will be mature. I will try to understand his feelings and know that they're valid. As valid as my own. Perhaps even more so. Even though a huge part of me wants to give him my fortune and take away all his troubles forever.

"I understand. I should *not* have offered to help you. I only wanted—"

He covers my lips with his fingers. "Don't say it. I know

what you're going to say. You only want to help. Use what you have to help the people you love. Don't you think I've heard Brock and Donny say the same things to Rory and Callie?"

I simply nod. My family may be rich, but we're also generous, and we gladly give to those we love.

"You see," he says, "I understand you think you love me, and God knows what I feel for you goes beyond even that—"

I open my mouth to respond, but again he quiets me.

"Yes, I know exactly what you're going to say. You're going to say you love me as much as I love you. And I want to believe that, Brianna. I do. And someday maybe I will. But my point is that my career and the band may finally be taking off. And you..." He shakes his head. "You... Well, you don't really fit into the plan."

My heart drops to my stomach, and a chill skitters down my spine.

It's not just sadness.

It's fear. Fear that Jesse may pull the plug on this whole thing.

"Yet I can't give you up," he goes on. "You're as essential to me as oxygen now. As the blood that runs through my veins. Without you, I'm a shadow of a man. At the risk of sounding very cliché, you complete me, Brianna."

I feel like I'm on a roller coaster, and each time I think I'm headed in one direction, the car twists and jolts me in another. "For God's sake, Jesse, you've got to throw me some kind of bone here. I don't know which end is up. You tell me I don't fit into your plans, but then you tell me I'm an essential part of *you*. You're pulling me in two directions. I don't know whether to be scared and sad or happy and elated."

He chuckles then, and I sit up, staring down at him.

"I don't see anything funny about that."

"Baby, I can laugh, or I can cry. It's not funny. It's just what it is. You talk about being pulled in two different directions. Don't you think I'm feeling the same thing? With my whole soul, I want to be a rock star. I want to take the band to true fame and fortune. And with my whole soul, I want to be with you and watch you fulfill your dreams as a rancher. How can I want both things so much when they're at odds with each other?"

CHAPTER NINETEEN

Jesse

My father taught me to play the guitar when I was only four years old. I took to it like a magnet to steel. I still have my first guitar—a small one to fit my childlike fingers. By the time I was eight, I had graduated to a full-size guitar. It was huge, and as my fingers grew, I made adjustments.

I got my first electric guitar when I was eleven. I loved that instrument. It was some knockoff brand, of course, but it was black with a white dragon on it. This was years before I met Dragon Locke. But even then, I was drawn to dragons.

I formed my first band in middle school. That's when Cage and I got together. Cage is a musical genius. He began playing the piano when he was only six, and when I approached him about forming a band, he took it upon himself to learn the bass guitar as well.

Someday maybe we'll have an actual bassist, but for now, Cage is able to handle the keyboard and the bass parts, using the keyboard of course.

We found Jake in high school. He was part of the jazz band that played at our football games. Our school wasn't large enough to have an actual marching band, so Jake's band played during the games. I, of course, was always on the field as the quarterback. Even from my freshman year, I was good enough to play varsity. Donny Steel and I were the only two freshmen on the varsity roster that year.

Cage didn't play football, so he joined the jazz band, and that's where he befriended Jake. Jake has a decent voice, but he's not lead vocal material. So we put him on lead guitar, and I was backup guitar. Our drummer at the time was Tomas Guzman. But Tomas moved away after graduation, so we needed a new drummer.

I went off to college in Wyoming on a football scholarship, and the band went on hiatus. We played when I was home on breaks, but without a drummer, we couldn't do much. After I graduated and came home for good to help on the ranch, I found Dragon at a local bar drumming for a house band.

And our band—known only as *the band* before then—finally had its name.

Dragon was quiet at first, but damn, he could play those drums like no one I knew. Tomas was talented, but Dragon made an art out of percussion. He was with the band for about a year before he opened up to me, and the only reason he did that was because we ended up on a gig on the eastern plains of Colorado, and he and I shared a room.

He swore me to secrecy, and I've never told a soul what he told me that night.

Why this is all swirling through my mind as I wait for Brianna to respond to my last statement boggles my mind. Then again, maybe the answer is clear as day. Remembering how our band came to be, how we've struggled for so many years, and how now we finally have the chance to take our career to the next level.

I can't let Brianna—or anything else—interfere with that. It's not just about me. It's about Cage and Jake. It's about Dragon, who unfortunately got involved with some bad women, but maybe it's a good thing, because now I know he'll never do that again. It's about Rory, my sister, who tried so hard for a career in opera but didn't make it. Who has now committed to rock and roll and has a chance to be the star I know she was born to be.

"Jesse," Brianna finally says, her voice soft and gentle, "we will find a way. We will find a way for both of us to live our dreams."

I sigh, shaking my head. "If only it were that simple."

"Nothing about life is ever simple," she says. "Even born to privilege like I've been, life hasn't been simple. It hasn't been simple for any of us." She sighs. "I could go on and on about what my family has been through. You know some of it, now that it's public knowledge."

She's right, of course. A lot of skeletons just emerged from the Steel family closet in the form of the late Wendy Madigan, who is Ryan Steel's birth mother. The older Steels knew about her, but it was news to the younger generation.

"Gina's having a really difficult time," Brianna goes on.

"I know. I understand. I'm sorry this is difficult for her."

And I want to understand. I do. But Gina Steel has a trust fund that's worth more than everything every member of my family owns put together. Her life won't change. In fact, nothing has changed. She thinks her genetics have changed, but her genetics were always what they were. She just didn't know.

Brianna pushes her hair behind her ear. "There are other things too, Jesse. Things I can't talk about. Things that aren't my stories to tell. But my father... And my brothers... They've been through hell that you can't even imagine."

Hell that *I* can't even imagine?

Dale Steel lost some of his vineyards. Our family lost *all* of ours.

But I don't want to quarrel with Brianna about the tough times of her family versus the tough times of mine. There are things she will never understand.

Which is probably why I fought these developing feelings so hard.

I've always found her attractive. In my mind, she's the most beautiful of all the Steel siblings and cousins. She's even more beautiful than her mother—who's the daughter of a supermodel.

But maybe I *need* to understand.

"Can you tell me a little bit?"

"I wish I could. I'm pretty sure Callie knows. Donny probably told her everything."

Donny Steel. My rival and my nemesis for so long. Now about to be my brother-in-law.

Perhaps my sister and I need to have a conversation. But if Bree and I are in love, shouldn't *she* be the one to tell me? I mean, if whatever she's talking about involves her father and her brothers, shouldn't that come from her? Not my sister?

But I choose to leave it.

I choose to leave it because I need a good night's sleep tonight. I have a concert tomorrow evening, rehearsal tomorrow afternoon.

The day after tomorrow, before we leave for Glasgow, the band and I will do some sightseeing in Edinburgh.

But tomorrow I have to be on.

I need to sleep well, and while I'm relaxed after making love with Brianna, now I'm thinking.

My mind is going a mile a minute, worrying about how I can keep the band on track and still deal with these massive emotions taking me over.

"If things work out between us, Brianna," I say, "I'm going to expect full honesty from you."

She bites her lower lip. "Before we get to any of that, don't you think we should figure out how to handle the rest of this tour? We need to tell the others."

"Do we? I don't want to mess this up for Maddie. And part of the deal with Maddie was that you would be there for her, rooming with *her*, seeing Europe with her."

She sighs. "I love Maddie. Truly I do. But Jesse... I want to be with you."

"That can't happen. All our reservations have already been made, and I'm rooming with Dragon. I only have this room to myself because he's still in London. You leaving Maddie for us to be together would put Maddie in a room with Dragon." I shake my head with a scoff. "And that is not happening in my lifetime."

I think of the talk I had with Dragon about his attempted seduction of Rory. And as protective as I am of Rory, I'm ten times more protective of Maddie, the baby of the family.

"But I need to be with you," she says.

I need to be with her too, probably more than she needs me. I'm still not convinced she feels for me what I've learned I feel for her. She thinks she does, but she's so young, and she's worshipped me from afar for so long.

She may not love me when she comes to know the real Jesse.

The Jesse who has secrets of his own. Secrets that may affect how she feels about me.

I should have kept my emotions at bay. I could have gotten her to agree to sleep with me for the duration of the tour to ease my tension, to keep me satisfied and focused at the same time.

But no... I had to go and blurt out that I'd fallen for her. That part of me had always wanted her.

"We can't. We'll be together as much as we can, but you need to stay with Maddie, and I need to stay with Dragon."

She nods.

"But we do have to tell them. Tomorrow at breakfast. Eight o'clock in the dining room."

She nods again and then she rises, grabs her jeans and sexy red thong off the floor, and begins to dress. "Can you at least walk me to my room?"

I'm a gentleman, and normally I would never hesitate at that request. But—

"What if Maddie sees me?"

"You just said we're going to tell them tomorrow anyway." She slides her red thong over her slim hips to cover that luscious pussy. Then she turns, giving me a bird's-eye view of her firm and shapely ass.

God, that ass. Licking her asshole. So many things I'm ready to do to her. So many things she may not be ready for.

Already my cock is getting hard again.

I could fuck her again. A quickie.

But no. We're both going to have to learn to keep our desires in check as the situation demands. We'll tell Maddie and the others tomorrow at breakfast. Donny and Callie are still in London, so at least I don't have to tell Donny Steel yet that I'm fucking his baby sister.

I let out a sarcastic chuckle. He's been fucking my sister for months.

Brianna turns and then sits back on the bed, sliding her feet into her jeans. "What's so funny?"

"Nothing."

Callie made Donny and me kiss and make up a while ago. My heart wasn't quite in it then, but I'm going to have to find it in myself now. Once they get married—and once Brock marries Rory—we will truly be family.

And damn...

If I can find a way to make this work with Brianna—a way where neither of us has to give up our dream—and if she truly does love me, if it's not just a puppy-love girlhood crush, if we can find a way to get through all that...

I may be more of a Steel family member than I ever thought I'd be.

"Of course I'll see you to your door. I'm sorry I got hesitant. I'm a gentleman, and I love you, Brianna. I will always see you to your door." I rise from the bed then as well and slide my jeans over my hips without bothering with my underwear.

I watch her continue to dress, and when she's finished, I ask, "You ready?"

Her jaw drops. "You don't have anything on."

I look down. My feet are bare, my chest is bare. "We're only walking down the hallway," I say.

"It's fine with me if it's fine with you."

But she's right. I haven't opened my suitcase yet, and digging out my slippers would be a pain. So I throw my shirt back on—which has no buttons now—and then my socks and boots.

Brianna gathers her purse and then goes to the bathroom for a minute, presumably to check her appearance. She comes back looking more beautiful than ever. Gorgeously *just fucked.*

And gorgeously *just Brianna.*

I walk her down the hallway to the room she shares with Maddie. It's late now, after midnight, and we have breakfast at eight.

"Where did you tell Maddie you were going?" I ask.

"I told her Brock needed to talk to me about some family stuff."

I frown. "Oh. I don't like you lying."

"I don't like it either. I want to be a good friend to Maddie, Jesse."

"I want that as well. That will be the last time you have to lie to my sister. We'll get this all out in the open at breakfast."

"Sounds good." She pulls out her key card.

I grab her then, give her a kiss.

Though I'm expecting it to be only a short kiss, she opens for me, and I dive in.

God... Kissing her...

A kiss with the hottest woman in the world in my fantasies was never this good.

Stop, Jess. Stop... You need to go to bed, need your sleep...

But I can't bring myself to break the kiss, and—

A screaming gasp pierces through the air.

And a breeze from the door opening.

"What the hell is going on here?"

CHAPTER TWENTY

Brianna

Jesse and I break our kiss simultaneously.

Instinctively I pull away from him, and my hand goes to my mouth, touching my swollen lips.

Maddie stands in the doorway of our room, wearing her lounging pants and tank top that she sleeps in. Her hair is in a braid behind her in the back, and she's wiping sleep out of her eyes.

Do I speak first?

Or should I let Jesse speak first?

We're both silent for what seems like an eternity until—

"Mads..." we both say in unison.

It would be comical if Maddie didn't look so horror-struck.

"I asked you point-blank." She waves her finger in my face. "I asked if you had designs on my brother, and you said you didn't."

"Maddie," Jesse says, "let us in. We'll explain everything."

"Fuck you both." She walks back in the room, slamming the door.

I hold up my key card. He nods at me, and then I hover it over the door, opening it. We walk in. Maddie is sitting on her bed.

"We were going to tell you everything in the morning," Jesse says.

"This doesn't change anything, Maddie," I say.

Maddie drops her jaw open. "Doesn't *change* anything? Are you fucking kidding me? This trip was supposed to be about you and me, Brianna. About our friendship. Not about you shacking up with my brother." Then she turns to Jesse, her eyes on fire. "And you? You've never given any one of the awesome foursome a look before. And now? It has to be now, when Brianna and I are supposed to be forging our friendship? Enjoying a trip to Europe together? Fuck you both."

"Maddie," I began, "I did lie to you, and I'm sorry. My feelings for Jesse are something I've had for a long time, and I never told anyone."

"That's another lie, Bree. I know you tell Gina, Angie, and Sage everything."

I shake my head. "Not this. It's something I've kept to myself since I was fourteen years old."

"You've been after my brother since you were fourteen years old?" She grimaces, and for a moment I think she's going to spit in my face. "You're disgusting."

"It started out as a crush," I say, "and if you're thinking badly of your brother, don't. He didn't know I was alive back then."

"Listen, Mads," Jesse says. "I didn't expect this to happen. But if you want me to be honest, I've always found Brianna very attractive. I never acted on it because I thought our age difference was too great. But... I don't know... Being in London and all..."

"You just couldn't help yourself?" Maddie scoffs.

"No, that's a lie," Jesse says. "It started before we left

Snow Creek."

He's talking about our kiss outside Murphy's.

So it *did* mean something to him.

I can't help a smile.

"And neither of you decided to tell me about it," she says.

"Because I didn't know what I was feeling," Jesse says.

"Sell it to someone who believes you." Maddie turns her back on us.

"Maddie," I say, "I should have been honest with you. I wanted to come on this tour because of Jesse. But I also wanted to come to experience it with you. I still do."

"Bullshit. You'd rather be sleeping with my brother."

She's not wrong, but Jesse and I can't stay together, and if I'm going to convince him that I love him as much as he professes to love me, I think it's better that we don't. It's better that we get to know each other more slowly.

He stays with Dragon, and I stay with Maddie. Maybe we can have a date here and there, if he has free time. And I'll let him use my body for all the tension release he needs. Because he's not really using me. Not now.

"I didn't expect this to happen, Mads," Jesse says. "But I'd be lying if I said it only started here in the UK. I began having feelings for Brianna before, though I lied to myself about it."

"This is really happening..." She turns toward us again, and this time her cheeks are streaked with tears. She sniffles. "Not only my two sisters, but now my brother has fallen for a Steel. Has gotten a Steel to fall for him. You're all going to be Steels, and where does that leave me?"

"Oh, Maddie." I sit down next to her, push her hair out of her face. "None of this changes anything."

"Brianna's right," he says. "Rory, Callie, and I are all Pikes first. That will never change, and all three of us will always be here for you."

"And Jesse and I are just beginning," I say. "We haven't talked about the future. I mean, I *hope* we have a future, but it's not something we're worried about right now. What's important right now is for Jesse and the band to give this tour everything they've got." I grab Maddie's hand. "I'm here for you, Maddie, and we're both here for them—to give them the support they need to make this tour everything they've ever dreamed of."

She sniffles back a sob. "That's all I want. For the band to be a success. For Mom and Dad's ranch and vineyard to be a success. And the success of the band can help that. I don't begrudge any of you finding love. Not the two of you, not Rory and Callie. But I'm always the odd one out. I'm not a true member of the awesome foursome, and now, I feel like the only Pike left."

"Didn't I just say that Rory, Callie, and I will always be Pikes first?"

"Yeah, you did. But I know how it is once you get married, Jesse."

"Brianna and I aren't getting married," Jesse says.

My heart breaks a little at that statement, but he's right. Our relationship is brand-new, and at the moment, our dreams seem to collide. There's no seem about it. They do collide. They explode.

I suck up my disappointment. "Your brother's right. He and I are new. I certainly hope it works out, but we haven't discussed it. Right now, we're just a new couple who found each other and fell in love. Nothing will change."

"This is why you didn't want me going off with Zane

Michaels, isn't it?" She turns to Jesse. "It had nothing to do with me. It's because you wanted Bree, so you ruined my night in the process."

"For Christ's sake." Jesse rakes his fingers through his hair. "It had everything to do with you. You're my sister, Maddie. No, I didn't want you going off with some playboy. No matter how good-looking or famous he is. No matter how rich he is."

"That is such a crock," Maddie says. "Rory and Callie are both engaged to two of the biggest playboys in our hometown, and they're just as rich as Zane Michaels, if not richer."

Maddie kind of has a point there. I'm not sure how Jesse will respond to that.

"That's different," he says, "and you know it. Donny and Brock have made commitments to Callie and Rory. They weren't just looking for one night with a hot groupie."

Nice job, Jesse. He handled that better than I expected. Especially since I know how he initially felt about both Donny and Brock dating his sisters. Especially Donny.

Maddie doesn't respond, which I take as a good thing. Jesse made sense to her.

"You're young, Maddie." I stroke her head again.

"I'm your exact age."

"You are. I'm young too. I just happened to find the man who I thought was my soulmate young, and it turns out he just might be."

"Rory was twenty-eight. Callie twenty-six," Jesse says. "You don't need to find someone at any certain age. It will happen when it happens."

She sniffles again. "Easy for both of you to say. Easy for Rory or Callie to say too."

"Look at the rest of the awesome foursome," I say. "Gina,

Angie, and Sage—they're all single. My sister, Diana, is twenty-five, and she's not in a relationship. This isn't a contest. It's not a race."

"Brianna's right," Jesse says. "It's not a race. It happens when it happens, whether you want it to or not."

"What's that supposed to mean?" she asks.

"I think what Jesse means," I say, my voice cracking slightly, "is that he wasn't expecting it to be me, and he wasn't expecting it to be now."

Jesse rubs his forehead. "Yeah, I figured that would piss you off. But you're absolutely right, Bree. That's exactly how it is for me. Now was not the best time for me to have found someone I want to be with. I need to focus on the band and the tour. But it happened. I can't say I'm not glad it happened. But the timing wasn't exactly perfection."

Again I hold back my disappointment at his words. "See, Maddie? You can't go around looking for it."

"You did," she says. "You came on this tour hoping to get my brother to fall in love with you."

"I came on this tour so I could be close to him. That's true. But I also came on this tour to be with you. And at the risk of beating a dead horse, Maddie, none of that has changed."

Jesse sighs. "I need to get to bed. And I want you two to get to bed as well. There's no more need to hash this out tonight, for either one of you. Brianna and I were planning to tell Brock and Rory in the morning, and we're still planning to do that. So, Maddie, I'll see you at breakfast." He gives me a chaste kiss on the cheek. "Good night, Bree."

"Good night, Jesse."

Jesse leaves, and I stroke Maddie's hair once more. "In the morning, this won't seem as weird to you."

"Don't bet on it." She sniffles.

I sigh, rise from her bed, and head toward my suitcase that's still standing against the wall. I open it, quickly find my pajamas, and head into the bathroom.

Tomorrow... Tomorrow we tell Brock and Rory.

And Rory will convince Jesse that we have to call Donny and Callie and tell them as well.

It's all fine with me.

But I know my brother will balk. He will balk, even though he is engaged to Jesse's sister. I can hear him already. "You're way too young, and Jesse, what the fuck are you doing with a twenty-two-year-old?"

Those are questions we're both going to have to be ready to answer, concerns we're going to have to be ready to refute. But tonight...

Tonight I'm still walking on air.

Because Jesse Pike—the man of my dreams—is in love with me.

Me.

And I'm going to float off to sleep on a pink cloud of love.

CHAPTER TWENTY-ONE

Jesse

Brianna and I sit at a round table in the dining room at the hotel with Maddie, who seems to be in a bit of a better mood after a good night's sleep. We're waiting for Brock and Rory to tell them about Brianna and me.

"You look good, sis," I say to Maddie.

"So you think I'm feeling better about all of this," she says.

"Hey, I just said you look good. Don't read anything into it."

"I'll deal," she says, waving me away with her fingers. "I've been dealing with being the odd one out for so long, it's second nature to me."

A little part of my heart breaks for my youngest sister. I know she's always felt left out among Brianna and her cousins.

"Maddie," Bree begins.

"Just stop it, both of you." Maddie sighs. "Neither of you will ever understand how I truly feel."

Bree opens her mouth but then closes it.

Good call.

I don't really think there's anything Brianna can say to make Maddie feel better. Brianna was raised in privilege, and Maddie was not. Hell, I was not.

So this is my load to haul.

"That's not exactly fair, Maddie," I say. "But I understand. You feel left out because you're the youngest. I've always felt left out too, not just because I'm the oldest, but because I'm the only guy in our family."

Maddie rolls her eyes. Yeah, I wasn't sure she would buy that. Being the only guy out of four children hasn't exactly been a hardship, especially since I'm the oldest.

"All right," I say. "So your two sisters are engaged. They're a lot older than you are. But Brianna and I are hardly engaged. Our relationship is just beginning. We don't know if it will be forever."

Brianna gnaws on her lower lip.

She's already decided this is forever.

I hope she's right. If it ends, it won't be because of me. I'm old enough to know that what I'm feeling for her is special, unique—something I never felt before even though I thought I was in love.

But she's young. Still so impressionable. And unfortunately, I may not be able to live up to the godlike image of me that she's created in her head.

If anyone ends up getting hurt in this relationship... I have a sinking feeling it won't be her.

Brock and Rory arrive, so I'm spared further rumination on the ultimate fate of Brianna's and my relationship.

Rory sits down, a smile on her face, until she looks at Maddie. "Mads, are you all right?"

Maddie simply shakes her head.

"What's wrong?" Rory asks.

"Ask your brother," Maddie says.

Rory scowls at me, and once Brock is sitting down next to Rory, I clear my throat. "We have some news for you guys."

Brock raises his eyebrows. "It's good news, I hope."

"I certainly think so," Brianna offers, her lips in a smile yet still trembling a bit.

I take Brianna's hand.

And Rory's jaw drops.

"What exactly is *this*?" Brock demands.

"Brianna and I... We've fallen in love."

Rory jumps out of her seat and comes around to the table, pulls me into a standing position, and gives me a big bear hug. "Jesse, this is amazing! How did I not see this coming?"

I pull back a bit, my eyebrows raised. "You're okay with it?"

"Of course. I just want you to be happy."

At least Rory is taking it well. "I didn't see it coming either, sis. But it hit me like a freight train."

Rory pulls Brianna up from her chair and hugs her too. She whispers something in Brianna's ear, but of course I can't hear it.

Then I move my gaze to Brock. His expression is different from his fiancée's.

The Steels... They don't like anyone touching their women. Well, too bad, how sad. Yes, Brianna's young, but the Steels took two of my sisters.

Once Rory is done effusing over Brianna and me, she glances toward Maddie again.

Our youngest sister isn't as thrilled about this match as Rory is, and Rory's noticing. She glances to me and then back to Maddie. For a minute I think Rory's going to say something, but she doesn't.

"When are you going to tell Donny?" Brock asks.

"Donny has nothing to say," I say. "He started things off with my sister."

Brock says nothing.

I know he's seething inside, despite the fact that he's with my sister and Donny's with another.

He knows there's nothing he *can* say.

"My brother will be just fine," Brianna says.

"And I think Callie will be thrilled," Rory offers.

Our server comes by and takes our breakfast orders, and once tea is poured for everyone, silence ensues.

"This is a happy occasion," Brianna finally says. "Everything is going to work out just fine."

Brock will come around. So will Donny. It's not like either of them have anything they can really say to me, considering they're both fucking my sisters.

But Maddie...

This whole thing is eating at my youngest sister. I wish I could fix it for her, but with getting the band through this tour, getting Dragon back on his feet, and my new relationship with Brianna...all my time is taken.

I'm going to have to rely on Brianna to take care of Maddie while I'm in rehearsal and onstage.

I believe she can do it. I believe she *will* do it. She made a promise to Maddie, and now that I'm in the picture, she won't want to disappoint me either.

But again my heart breaks just a little as I gaze at my youngest sister, her pretty face so sad.

"Maddie, can I talk to you in private for a moment?" I ask.

She rises. "Sure, what the heck?"

I lead her away, toward the elevators, out of earshot of Brock, Rory, and Brianna, who are still at the table.

"Hey," I say. "What can I do to fix this for you?"

She crosses her arms. "You can't fix it. And I wouldn't ask

you to."

"There's got to be something I can do. Or something Rory or Callie can do."

"Callie's still in London."

"True."

"It's just..." She looks up at me, her dark eyes misty. "I thought Brianna and I were getting close. But all she wanted was you, Jesse."

Maddie's words could be true for all I know—at least initially. But now I believe that Brianna is more than that. That Brianna is a friend too—a good friend.

"I think that might have been her original reason for wanting to go on the tour," I admit. "But she wants to make this special for you, sis. And I'd like to make it special for both of you. I'll be tied up with the band for the majority of the time. Brianna and I won't have the chance to do much sightseeing together. That's where you come in. You and Brock. Once Donny and Callie go back to the States, it'll just be you three to see the rest of Europe."

"Bree will just be wishing she was with you."

"First, I don't think that's the case. Brianna knew full well when she came on this tour that I would be busy. That I wouldn't be doing much sightseeing. Second, she made a commitment to you, and I believe she will keep it. The Steels may have their faults, but they see their commitments through to the end. They're trustworthy, and you can depend on them."

Maddie huffs. "Nice change of tune, Jess. You never trusted the Steels a day in your life, and now all of a sudden you fall for one and everything's fine?"

"It's not that I didn't trust them," I say, "though I get why you would think that. I've just always been...envious, to be honest. Everything comes so easy for them. They were born into a perfect life. But what we see as outsiders isn't always the case. The Steels have their own problems, and I see that now. I also see their generosity, and it took me a while, but I'm doing better at accepting what they offer."

"Right."

"It still stings. I won't lie to you, Mads. But I do think they're trustworthy. I know Brianna is."

"You think you know her better than I do?"

"In some ways."

She makes a face. "Gross, Jesse."

"I don't mean like that." I shake my head. "Brianna isn't going to let you down, and neither am I."

She sniffles but finally nods.

"Come on back to the table. Eat your breakfast. I understand that you, Brianna, and Brock have a guided tour of part of Edinburgh this morning."

"Yeah, we do."

"Then be happy. You're in Scotland, Mads. You're going to see your brother and sister perform tonight, but before that, you're going to have a wee good time."

My ridiculous attempt at a Scottish brogue finally gets a smile out of her.

"Are you sure?" she asks.

"Sure about what? That you're going to have a great time? Absolutely."

"No. Are you sure you love Brianna?"

"I am," I say without even thinking about it. "It came on me hard and fast, but I think it was always there. I just refused to see it. Didn't want to see it. Didn't think it could ever work with her."

"Because of her age?"

"That, yes. But also because she's a cowgirl. A rancher at heart, like her father and uncles. And I'm a rocker. A musician. I have to travel to sing for my supper." I shake my head. "Part of me still doesn't know how we're going to get over that hump. But I'm not going to think about it too much. We're here now. I have to make this tour work. Brianna's here, and we can be together at least part of the time. I have to get through this tour, Mads. I have to make it a success. I'll worry about the rest of it later."

CHAPTER TWENTY-TWO

Brianna

Later that morning, I get a text from Brock saying that he needs to stay at the hotel to work on some business.

"I guess it's just you and me for the Edinburgh tour, Mads," I say cheerfully.

She sighs. "I guess."

"Buck up." I grab her hand as we get into our cab that will take us to the starting point for the tour.

It's a premium tour on a luxury bus with an actual tour guide and all. We had one tour in London like that, but the rest of the time we checked out the sights ourselves.

Once on the bus, our tour guide, a man named Ferdie—dark-haired, blue-eyed, and sporting a kilt—speaks through the microphone in a fun Scottish accent.

"Our first stop will be Edinburgh Castle," Ferdie announces. "The castle is perched on Castle Rock and has witnessed centuries of history and offers breathtaking panoramic views of the city. You'll have the opportunity to explore the Crown Jewels, the Stone of Destiny, and learn about the castle's role in Scotland's history."

A few moments later, the bus stops. "Ladies and gentlemen," Ferdie says, "as you approach the castle, you'll walk along the Esplanade, which is a large open space in front of the main entrance. This is the site of the famous Royal Edinburgh Military Tattoo during the month of August."

"The bagpipe thing?" someone asks.

"Yes, the bagpipe thing." Ferdie laughs. "But the Tattoo features more than just pipes. They host a wide variety of military bands, pipe and drum corps, and other performance groups from different countries. If you can get back here in August, it's something you don't want to miss."

I'm not big on pipes and drums, but I bet Jesse would love the Tattoo. Maybe he and I will come back here in August.

I stop myself.

Totally putting the cart before the horse, as my father likes to say.

We leave the bus, and Ferdie is still speaking to us through a wireless mic as we stroll toward the castle. "We'll enter the castle through the Portcullis Gate, a fortified entrance with a large wooden drawbridge."

"How can it have a drawbridge?" someone asks. "Isn't that to let ships through?"

"It's no longer a functional drawbridge," Ferdie replies with a chuckle.

The man reddens. "Right."

"Portcullis Gate leads you into the heart of the castle complex," Ferdie continues. "Once you're inside, you'll be on your own to explore for an hour. One of the highlights is the Crown Jewels of Scotland, including the crown, scepter, and sword that are used in various royal ceremonies."

"Are they different from England's Crown Jewels?" a young woman asks.

"They are, though they're still the property of the reigning monarch of the United Kingdom. And they're considered priceless. You'll also find the Stone of Destiny, an ancient symbol of Scottish monarchy. Don't miss the Great Hall—a magnificent space adorned with armor and weaponry, showcasing Scotland's martial history."

I giggle. Ferdie sounds like a robot. I'm sure he's given this same speech hundreds of times.

"St. Margaret's Chapel is one of the oldest surviving structures in Edinburgh," Ferdie continues. "Mons Meg is a massive medieval siege cannon located on the castle grounds. It's an impressive piece of artillery that provides insight into the castle's military history. If you have time, check out the National War Museum, which offers an extensive collection of artifacts, documents, and exhibitions covering Scotland's military history. There are a few other sights you might want to see as well. Grab a brochure from me, and we'll meet back here in one hour."

Maddie and take our brochures from Ferdie and enter the castle.

I stop in awe, again wishing Diana were here. As an architect, she'd appreciate this wondrous structure far more than I ever could. All I can do is gape at its beauty and majesty. Maddie and I hit everything Ferdie recommended—the Crown Jewels of Scotland were so beautiful—and are about to hit the National War Museum when my phone buzzes.

I have a text...and I notice the time. Our hour is up, and we have to get back to the entrance to meet Ferdie and the rest of the group.

"Mads, we have to go."

"Already?"

"Yeah. Plus I have a text from Brock."

"Is everything okay?"

I glance at the text quickly. "Yeah, but he wants us to get back for lunch."

"But our tour includes lunch."

"I know." I tap out a message into the phone.

On a tour with Maddie. Includes lunch.

The three dots move, and...

Okay. Never mind. Finish your tour.

What's up?

Nothing urgent. Just some changes in our seating for the concert. I'll talk to you when you get back to the hotel.

"Apparently our seating for the concert has changed," I tell Maddie. "Not sure why he needed to tell us that in person."

"Who knows?" Maddie says. "We'd better get back before Ferdie leaves without us."

We walk swiftly out of the castle until we finally reach the entrance. Ferdie is standing in front of the group, his arms crossed.

"I was going to give you two lassies one more minute." He clicks his tongue at us.

"We're sorry," I say. "We were enjoying the castle. That crown is magnificent."

"I'm glad you enjoyed your time. Let's go. We're going to walk the Royal Mile that connects the castle to Holyrood Palace."

Maddie and I glance at each other, and Maddie chuckles.

Good. She's been somber since getting the news about Jesse and me.

"What?" I ask.

"He sounds like a recording," she says.

"I was thinking the same thing during his speech about the castle. He seemed annoyed when people asked questions. I'm sure he's said these things about a million times." I glance around. The man standing next to me is wearing an Emerald Phoenix T-shirt. "Hey," I say to him.

He holds out his hand. "I'm Willie."

"Brianna. You like Emerald Phoenix?"

"Love them. Got tickets to the concert tonight. Will you be there?"

"I will!" I gush. "And you'll love—"

Willie's eyes go wide, and he opens his mouth to say something, but Ferdie interrupts us through the microphone.

"A walk along the Royal Mile is a journey through the heart of Edinburgh's Old Town, offering a mix of history, architecture, shops, and culture. It's a cobblestone street that stretches approximately one mile—hence the name—from Edinburgh Castle to Holyrood Palace. As you explore, you'll pass by various landmarks and charming spots, including a visit to St. Giles' Cathedral. We'll begin our walk at Castlehill, where I'll give you twenty minutes to take in the souvenir shops."

"Souvenir shops?" Maddie shakes her head. "I'd rather have had the extra twenty minutes in the castle."

"Yeah, me too."

"Me three," Willie says. "You ladies mind if I join you?"

Maddie wrinkles her forehead. "Uh...who are you,

exactly?"

"He's a fan of Emerald Phoenix," I say. "Oh! I was going to tell you. My boyfriend—her brother—is the lead singer of the opening band. Dragonlock."

"He's the co-lead singer," Maddie corrects me. "My sister Rory also sings lead vocals."

Willie's eyes go wide. "You mean you two know Emerald Phoenix?"

"We do," I say.

"Wow. I mean...wow!"

Willie is tall and handsome, and Maddie appears to take notice. "I'm Maddie." She smiles shyly.

"Is that short for Madison?" he asks.

"Madeline," she says. "And Willie's short for William?"

"I wish." He grimaces. "Willard, actually."

I let myself walk behind Willie and Maddie as the tour heads on to Lawnmarket, which is lined with colorful shops, cafés, and historic buildings, all of which Ferdie describes in excruciating detail. I appreciate it for sure, but the droning is getting tiresome. Besides, I truly wish I were back at the castle with more time.

Maddie and Willie hang out for the rest of the tour, including our stop for lunch in Old Town, where we feast on brisket, neeps, and tatties—Scots speak for turnips and potatoes. But I don't begrudge Maddie anything. I'm glad she found someone to give her some attention.

The tour is educational and fun, but by the time it ends, I'm missing Jesse so much I can taste it. I know he's busy rehearsing and preparing for the concert, but I can't help hoping that he's missing me too, if only just a little.

CHAPTER TWENTY-THREE

Jesse

After a good rehearsal, I get a call from Callie when I'm back in my room. "Hey, sis. Everything okay?"

"Hey... Yeah. Dragon's doing really well..."

My heart sinks at her tone. "I'm sensing a *but* coming."

She sighs through the phone. "Yeah... His doctors think he should go home. Get into a rehab program."

"For fuck's sake." I rub my jawline.

"I know. But here's the thing. Dragon agrees."

"He *what*?"

"Yeah. He doesn't want to let you guys down, and—"

"For fuck's sake," I say again. "Just put him on the phone, will you?"

Callie sighs again. "He doesn't want to talk to you, Jess."

"Well, he's going to. Put him on the damned phone."

I hear the shuffling through the line, and then—

"Hey, Jess."

"Dragon, what the fuck?"

"Look. The reason I didn't want to talk to you is because I knew you would try to talk me out of this." He pauses. "But I need to be honest with you, Jesse. I don't want to let you down again, and I think the best thing for me to do is to go home, get into a serious rehab, and never fucking take a drink or smoke a joint again."

"You've been clean for over five years."

"Yeah. Except for the booze and the pot. I always thought I could handle it, but I want to be clean for good, Jesse. I don't ever want this to happen to me again."

"What exactly are you saying, Dragon?"

Silence for a moment that seems like an eternity, and already I know what's coming. Damn him.

Damn the motherfucker for lying to me.

And damn myself for fucking believing him.

"I didn't remember a lot of that night for a while, but slowly, things started coming back. I started to remember through the haze."

Count to ten, Jesse. Fucking count to ten.

"It was tough at first," he continues, his voice cracking. "Like I thought I was dreaming, and I wasn't sure what was real, but now I'm sure." Another pause. "I lied to you, Jesse. Those women didn't drug me. I took the stuff."

Anger curls through me, at myself and at Dragon. Fucking Dragon...

Count to ten, Jesse. Count to—

"I trusted you, man!" I yell into the phone.

Silence again, until—

"I know you did. I swear to God, I will make this up to you. But you guys are better off without me on this tour. I'm going to get clean, man. Totally. So clean that I'll never be tempted again."

Count to fucking ten, Jesse!
One...
Two...
Three...

"You going to say anything, Jess? Or are you so pissed you can't speak?"

Fuck, he has no idea.

"Dragon," I say, taking care to regulate my voice despite my anger. "You're an addict, man. You're always going to be tempted."

"Yeah. But I think I can get a handle on it. I thought I had a handle on it. But I—"

Rage surges through me. Fuck counting to ten. "I can't believe you, Dragon! This was our big shot. You almost blew it for us. And now I'm going to have to see if I can get Derek to sub in for you for the entire tour. He's a great drummer, but he's kind of an asshole. Totally rubs me the wrong way. Plus, how does that make us look with Emerald Phoenix? We look like fucking amateurs."

I'm not exactly being fair. A lot of professionals have drug problems.

And the money to support them.

But I don't give a rat's ass about any of that in this moment. I trusted him. I trusted Dragon. He told me he was drugged, and I believed him. I didn't even hesitate because I trusted him beyond all else. After everything we've been through together. After everything he's been through. How *could* he?

The stories he's told me flash through my mind. He's had a tough life. Tougher than I can even think about.

But this tour means everything to all of us. Not just me, but Cage, Jake, and Rory. For my fucking family.

"For God's sake, Dragon, we named the fucking band after you."

"Jesse, I'm not leaving the band. I just need to do this. For myself. And for you guys. But I'd sure understand if you kick me out. Hell, I'd probably kick me out if I were you."

"Dragon, damn it—"

"It's me, Jess." My sister's voice.

"Callie, put him back on."

"This is why he didn't want to talk to you. He knew you wouldn't take it well. But Donny and I have talked to his doctors, and we agree with Dragon that this is what's best."

"You and Donny don't have a clue what's at stake here."

My sister huffs. "You don't think I know what's at stake here? I'm your sister, Jesse. I've watched you work your ass off to make a go at this band, and I understand that this is your big chance. But you have another drummer, and you said yourself he's excellent."

"He only agreed to drum for us during the UK part of the tour." I leave out the part that he's kind of a dick.

"Jesse…"

"What am I supposed to tell the rest of the band? That Dragon just checked out on us? That he fucking lied to my face? That he took not only fentanyl but also let those bitches roofie him?"

"Jess, he took the Rohypnol too. He took it all knowingly. At least that's what he finally remembers."

"For fuck's sake." I hurl the phone at the wall.

I breathe in, trying to get my bearings. Then I pick up the phone.

"You there?" I demand.

"I'm here. Stop acting like a child, Jesse. You tell the band that Dragon and his doctors feel this is the best call for now."

I shake my head. Rub my fingers through my hair.

I hope Derek is up for subbing in for the rest of the tour. I hope Jett is up for it too. After all, Emerald Phoenix pays their backup drummer's bills, but the pay goes up if he has to actually go onstage.

"Callie, he's making us look like a bunch of amateurs."

"He feels terrible."

"I don't fucking care how he feels right now."

"I'm surprised at you. Dragon told me personally that you of all people would understand."

"You know? Maybe I would have. But he lied to me, Callie. He told me they drugged him. Besides, there's a difference between understanding what Dragon has been through and understanding what's at stake here for the band."

"I know." Callie pauses a moment. "But here's the thing, Jess. No band is ever more important than the people who make it up."

My anger dissipates a little then...but only a little. He still lied to my face, and I'm not sure I can forgive that...no matter what he and I have been through together. Sure, he said he didn't remember, but—

"We've made arrangements for Dragon to travel home with us, after your encore concert back in London. Dragon wanted to stay and see the concert."

"Dragon should be *onstage* for that concert."

"No, he shouldn't." Callie's voice changes, becoming sterner. "He let you down, and he knows it. What he wants now is for the tour to go on as planned. It's killing him not to be up there with you guys, but he feels this is the best move for the band and for himself."

I want to shout back at her through the phone, but I stop myself. What good would it do anyway? What's done is done. Dragon fucked up. Nothing can change that now. If I'd been with him, though...instead of fucking Brianna...

He wouldn't have taken the drugs.

But I'm not going back there. He's a damned grown-up.

"Fine. I suppose I should thank you and Donny for taking care of him."

After all, the two of them did give up their travels in the UK so the band could go on and Maddie and Brianna could continue with their travels.

"We were glad to do it. This concert means just as much to me as it does to you and Rory."

"I know."

"Try to understand, okay?"

I sigh. "I can't help it. I'm angry. Angry that he would do this. That he would take drugs. Put the band in jeopardy during our big chance."

"You're not as angry as he is with himself. He's absolutely distraught. And he realizes he needs help. He's going to make it, Jesse. He *wants* to make it, but he's going to need your support. He's more upset at himself for lying to you than he is for taking the damned drugs. Let me tell him he has your support. Please."

"Tell him whatever you need to tell him, Cal. But it'll take me some time to come to grips with this."

"I know. I'm sorry it falls to you to tell Rory and the guys about this."

"I just hope we can get Derek to fill in for the rest of the tour."

"I hope you can too. But if you can't, Donny and I have already decided that we'll find you another drummer who can go on tour. Money is no object."

"For God's sake."

"Shut up, Jesse. Just shut up right now. Donny's money is my money, and we're doing this. You will have your drummer, no matter what."

There's not much else I can say. I already know I can get Derek. He made it clear that he'd join the band if we ever kicked Dragon to the curb. It's almost like he knew something like this would happen. Maybe he just knows what addiction is like.

I have to assume he's on the up and up because we need him.

I'll get his bills paid one way or another, even if it's with Steel money.

I have to.

For the band.

★ ★ ★

Brianna and I decided not to see each other before the concert. She did text me to tell me she had a wonderful time on her guided tour today with Maddie.

Rory, Cage, and Jake took the news about Dragon better than I did.

"To be honest, Jess," Cage said, "I always thought he was our weak link. I mean, as a percussionist he's perfection, but there was always that part of me that wondered if he would relapse."

Both Rory and Jake nod.

I didn't bother trying to defend Dragon. I didn't bother telling them how much I always trusted him.

Doesn't matter now anyway.

The talk with Derek wasn't as agreeable.

"I've got to say I'm not surprised, brother," he said after I told him Dragon wouldn't be returning for the rest of the tour.

I'm not your fucking brother.

I didn't say that, of course. "We're in a bind now, and we'd be obliged if you'd continue with the tour."

"Absolutely. Happy to. But we'll have to talk money. Jett only agreed to the UK portion."

"I know, and if it's all right with you, I'd rather not drag Jett into this. I feel bad enough that everything didn't go as planned from the outset."

"I get it, man. But lesson learned, you know? You can't trust an addict."

One, two, three, four...

"What will it take?" I ask. "Whatever you need, and it's yours. My sisters' fiancés will take care of the money."

"Not a problem," he said. "Brock and I have already come to terms."

I shake my head. I don't even want to know. "Great. Glad you're on board."

After that, Rory, Cage, Jake, and I had a light dinner, and now we're at the venue, sound check is completed, and we're about ready to have our moment of silence before we take the stage once more with Derek.

I close my eyes.

God, give us the strength and perseverance to rock this concert, to stay in sync, to give the audience our best. And about Dragon...

I do something I never do. I open my eyes before I'm done.

The other four, including Derek, still have their eyes closed. I close my eyes and continue.

Thank you for finding us a talented drummer. Help my attitude about him. And please watch over Dragon, and help me see this as an opportunity for him rather than a loss for the band.

Help me regain my trust in him, and help him to be worthy of my trust. Thank you for this opportunity, for Emerald Phoenix, for Rory and the band, and also for Brianna. It may not be forever, but it seems to be what we both need for now.

I open my eyes, and that last thought—of Brianna—disappears.

Only the concert matters now.

We end with our one, two, three...Dragonlock!

We take the stage. The lights stream onto us. Percussion, and then guitar, and then Cage on his keys.

Rory and I sing.

And we fucking rock.

CHAPTER TWENTY-FOUR

Brianna

The change in our seating that Brock mentioned turns out to be in the third row instead of the first row that we were expecting. Emerald Phoenix had a rash of VIPs who they didn't know would attend until the last minute. Turned out okay, though, as Willie from our tour showed up and was seated next to Maddie. He had a backstage pass, and he and Maddie were chatting up a storm last I saw.

"Who is that?" Jesse asks me.

"That's Willie. Maddie and I met him when we toured the castle. We had lunch together."

"I don't like the way he's looking at her. Or at you."

I wrinkle my brow. "Seriously? He hasn't given me a look. Besides, I made it clear to him that I had a boyfriend."

"I don't want him looking at Maddie like that either."

"He's harmless," I say. "He's here because he's a huge Emerald Phoenix fan. He was wearing an EP T-shirt during our tour."

Jesse's eyes don't stray from him and Maddie, though, until I tug on his arm.

"Let's get out of here."

That softens him, and Jesse and I leave from the concert together.

Maddie knows about us. And Zane Michaels is staying far away from her tonight.

Jesse makes his obligatory nods to fans and to the members of Emerald Phoenix, and then he and I leave quietly. Brock and Rory have promised to see that Maddie gets safely back to the hotel—without Willie.

Jesse says nothing. Simply leads me to his room, opens it with this key card, and then pulls me inside. In a flash I'm against the wall, my hands above my head, secured by his wrists. His mouth comes down on mine, and he plunders me with a kiss.

His body is hot, and his hair is slicked back with sweat. From his performance? No. His performance was over before Emerald Phoenix's began.

No. He's hot for me.

I melt into his kiss, my body becoming jelly. If my wrists weren't secured by his strong hands at the wall, I would float into a puddle on the floor.

We kiss for... I don't know how long...

All I know is the ecstasy becomes nirvana, and I'm under the complete thrall of Jesse Pike.

I know I'm in for a fast fuck. It's what he does after concerts. It's what he needs.

Which makes what he did for me when he took my virginity that much more special.

When he finally rips his mouth from mine, I gasp in a much-needed breath of air.

"Damn, Brianna..." His voice is a low snarl. He's still holding me up, my arms above my head. "I need to fuck you. I need to be inside you. I need my cock inside your tight pussy. It's not going to be sweet, Brianna. It's not going to be nice or gentle. It's going to be an animal fuck. I'm going to rut inside you, Brianna."

"I..." But I have no words.

If he fears his words will turn me off, he's wrong.

I like when he's an animal. When he's a wolf. When he's a fucking dragon, breathing fire.

Dragon may be the band's namesake, but Jesse is the real dragon. That mythical creature with the strength and fortitude of an ancient beast representing power, protection... and sometimes chaos and destruction.

That is Jesse Pike. A man with a goal. A man who's worked hard all his life to become the musician he knows he can be.

All that strength and perseverance, all that integrity and fortitude.

With a little chaos on the side. An amazing combination.

I may have been attracted to him because of his gorgeous looks, but that's not what made me fall in love with him.

I fell in love with a man who was determined to make it. Whose fierce determination overruled everything else in his life. And who—whether the audience is one person or a whole fucking stadium full—always gives each performance everything he's got.

And this fuck he's about to give me? It's just another type of performance. And I know he'll give me everything he's got.

"You're so fucking beautiful," he growls.

"I want to be beautiful for you. Only you."

"Good. Because when other men look at you, all I can think about is that you're mine. That no one will ever touch you but me."

Strong words from a man who hasn't yet made a commitment to me. But love itself is a commitment. Perhaps that's what he means.

He releases my arms then, and I drop them to my sides, shaking them to release the tension. He cups the back of my neck so my head tilts back, and I meet his fiery gaze.

"Mine," he says again.

And then he kisses me again, his tongue devouring my mouth as I grip his shoulders and then wrap one arm around his neck, threading my fingers through his silky hair and tugging gently.

His groan vibrates into me, and my whole body feels it, like subtle quakes and quivers from my head to my toes.

With one hand, he cups my breast, squeezing it. We're both still fully clothed, yet I feel close to him. So close. As if we're one already.

He breaks the kiss quickly and sucks in a breath. "Bed," he growls.

All I can do is nod, my body trembling with desire.

He turns but then seems to rethink that, and he sweeps me into his arms and carries me to the bed. He lays me down—not gently—and then pulls off my cowboy boots and my socks. Next, he takes care of my jeans and thong and then my tank and bra.

When I'm lying in front of him, my nipples hard and my pussy wet, he simply stares at me.

"You're a fucking dream," he says with a rasp. "The most gorgeous thing on this planet, Brianna. That's what you are."

I can't help a small smile with my trembling lips. "Please, Jesse. Please..."

He removes his shoes and socks quickly, and then begins to unbuckle his belt. He wore the dragon tonight.

His black T-shirt still covers his gorgeous chest, but at

this point, I just want him inside me. We can get to the T-shirt later. The clank of the belt buckle, and then the zip of his jeans. In another second, they're over his hips, and he pulls me by my legs to the edge of the bed, plunging into me with a groan.

I cry out—not from pain but from sheer pleasure at having my heart's desire fulfilled.

This is no longer simply physical. It's emotional, yes, but also spiritual. Already I'm on my way to the heavens. He thrusts so hard that he hits my clit with his pubic bone each time.

I grab the comforter, arching my back, and closing my eyes as I climb and climb and climb...

"Jesse!"

"God yes, come for me. Come for me. I own those orgasms, Brianna. Only for me."

He continues devouring my pussy with his cock, faster, faster, faster...

And when he pushes in, releasing, I catapult into yet another orgasm.

We come in synchrony. In perfect harmony, and I swear to God, it's the most beautiful feeling I've ever experienced.

He collapses on top of me, bearing his weight on his arms as he brushes his lips over mine. "Do you remember the night I took your virginity?"

He's seriously asking me that? It was only a few nights ago. "Of course I do. I'll never forget it." I sigh.

"I'm going to make love to you like that again, only it's going to be so much better. It won't always be like this, Brianna. It won't always be a quick hard fuck because I need to release after a performance."

I fold my hands behind my head and stare into his

gorgeous dark smoldering eyes. "I'm not exactly complaining."

He rises then, pulls out of me, and sheds his jeans and T-shirt. He lies back down next to me, our flesh in total contact.

He feels perfect against me, and I snuggle up to his shoulder, absently playing with the black curls on his chest.

"When did you fall in love with me?" I ask.

"I don't know how to answer that question."

"Why?"

"Because there's no easy answer. I've been attracted to you for so long, but I didn't let myself feel anything. You already know why. Because of the age difference, and because you're a Steel. But in the last couple of months, without meaning to, I opened myself up. Maybe it's because both my sisters fell for a Steel, and I saw a side of the Steels that I hadn't let myself see before."

I can't help a chuckle. "That we're not a bunch of privileged assholes?"

"I never thought you were assholes."

"But you *did* think we owned the whole town."

"I grew up thinking that. Everyone thought it, Bree. It was kind of like the town motto."

I scrunch my nose. "A motto? More like the town slur."

"I can see how you would think of it that way, but it wasn't really meant to be disparaging. It was simply accepted as truth, and then, when it bit me in the ass—by Donny getting MVP instead of me senior year—I began to take it more seriously. I began to resent the hell out of your family."

I open my mouth to refute his words, but he holds up his hand to stop me.

"I no longer feel that way, Brianna. Besides, now it's been sorted."

"True enough," I say. "It was actually Wendy Madigan who owned the town."

"A surprise to all of us. But what I never understood was why there wasn't a lien from Wendy on the Pike property."

"We may never know," I say. "Does it matter? Everything worked out."

Jesse sighs. "I have a lot of questions. Questions I'm probably going to demand answers to from your father and his brothers."

My heart sinks a little. But I can't fault Jesse.

"But they're not here, and right now, holding you, those questions don't seem all that important."

I smile against his shoulder. "I'm glad you feel that way."

He kisses my forehead. "I should get you back to your own room."

"Will I see you tomorrow?"

"As a matter of fact, you will. I'm going to accompany you, Maddie, Brock, and Rory to the Museum of Scotland in the morning, and then in the afternoon, I made arrangements just for you and me to go to the whisky experience."

"Really?" I jerk up in bed. "I didn't know you liked Scotch."

"I drank it our first night here, if you recall."

That's right. He did. He ordered a Scotch...before we... Heat floods to my cheeks.

I smile. "I'm a bourbon girl myself, like my father, but Scotch is its own experience. It's so different from other whiskeys. That's so nice of you to think of that for me. It's something I would love to do."

"That's why I thought of it. Brock, Rory, and Maddie have no interest in it. I asked them. When they said no, I couldn't help but be happy." He smiles, cups my cheek. "Because that,

Brianna, will be our first official date."

CHAPTER TWENTY-FIVE

Jesse

I'm not a museum kind of guy, but the National Museum of Scotland wasn't a complete bore, and Brianna seemed to love it. She walked with wide eyes through all the exhibits, especially the natural history displays. She's a girl of the land for sure, and again I was reminded how I can't take her away from her future—working her family's land. I enjoyed the art and design exhibits—especially Rembrandt and Vermeer—but I was disappointed that there weren't any exhibits pertaining to the music of Scotland.

After lunch at a nearby café, Brianna and I head to the whisky experience. The Scotch Whisky Experience is situated right next to the entrance of the Edinburgh Castle, and Brianna talks nonstop about the castle's beauty and grandeur. It's a gorgeous building for sure.

"I wish you could have been with Maddie and me yesterday," she says animatedly. "We almost missed our bus back because we were loving the castle so much. I kept thinking about how Diana would love to be here and experience all the architecture."

Another reminder of what Brianna and I *don't* have in common. The castle is gorgeous, to be sure, but I tend to live in the present, not in the past. History—other than music and art—doesn't interest me much, so I doubt I would have had any issue with being back on time to meet the tour group. My littlest sister, though, loves history and culture...and apparently so does Brianna.

I tuck the thought in the back of my mind. No need to dwell on how Brianna and I will never work in the long term. I arranged this whisky tour for her, and I plan for both of us to enjoy it.

The whisky experience has its own address and everything. These people take their whisky seriously. I'm surprised when a young man greets us.

"Welcome!" he says. "My name is George, and it's my pleasure to guide you through your experience today."

He's tall and blond, and I don't particularly like the way he looks at Brianna.

"We didn't sign up for a tour," I say, not smiling.

"You don't have to," he says. "We offer guides to individuals and groups to help you get the most out of the experience."

"We don't need a—"

Brianna tugs on my arm. "Let's go with him, Jesse. He'll make sure we get the most out of this."

"I'm happy to oblige, pretty lassie," George says.

I raise an eyebrow at him. I'm not sure he gets the hint. "Fine," I say dryly.

"We'll start with the whisky barrel ride," George begins. "It's a simulated ride that takes you through a virtual tour of the whisky-making process, from the barley fields to the distillery and beyond."

"How exciting!" Brianna's eyes are wide.

George guides us to barrel-shaped seats. Seriously, barrel shaped. I feel like I'm in an amusement park. Was this really my idea? Brianna somehow ends up in the middle of us as George lowers the safety bar. The lights dim, and our barrel pushes forward.

This is so not what I had in mind.

I thought Brianna and I would taste different whiskies, not be shoved into Edinburgh's version of *Pirates of the Caribbean*.

I need an attitude adjustment, but apparently that part of the experience happens later.

Despite myself, however, I find the tour interesting. We "travel" through the various stages of whisky production, including mashing, fermentation, distillation, and maturation, though the "scenic views" of the Scottish countryside pale in comparison to the real thing. Not that I've seen much of the countryside, nor will I, as we leave for Glasgow tomorrow. I guess I'll see it through the train window.

The ride takes about twenty minutes.

"I hope you enjoyed that immersive experience," George says.

"Yes, it was fabulous!" Brianna gushes. "When do we taste?"

Ah, yes... Brianna is my girl.

George laughs. "You like whisky, then?"

"I like bourbon," she says. "I don't know a lot about Scotch, but I've had it a few times back home."

"Where are you from?"

"The US."

"I know that, lassie. Where in the States?"

"Oh. Sorry. Colorado. The western slope."

"I see. I doubt you've had much good whisky. Or Scotch, as you yanks say. You're in for a treat."

Brianna takes George's comment in stride, but clearly he

doesn't know who he's talking to. Bree and her family drink only the best liquor.

We enter a room filled with an extensive collection of whiskies from different regions of Scotland.

"Here are the diverse range of whisky brands and styles, each representing the distinct characteristics of its region," George says. "There's single malt and single grain whisky. Malt whiskies are complex and smoky, while grain tends to be lighter and sweeter. In the States, you've probably tasted single malt whisky."

"Maybe," Brianna says. "Jesse?"

"I don't have a clue," I say dryly.

"We'll taste one of each," George says. He leads us to a bar where several bottles stand. "Have a seat."

Once we're seated, George pours each of us a glass of amber liquid. "This is a single malt from the Highlands of Scotland. Swirl it around in your glass and capture the aroma."

Brianna swirls like an expert. I feel foolish. Still, I swirl and sniff. Hmm... Not bad. It smells almost...floral. Weird.

"Now taste it," George says. "Let it sit on your tongue for a moment before you swallow. It should feel velvety in your mouth."

Brianna takes a sip and holds it. I do the same but swallow right away. Ugh. Not impressed. Though I enjoyed the scent, the flavor is kind of like dirt.

"Well?" George asks.

"Delicious," Brianna says. "Mossy and peaty. With a slight... I don't know. A flower of some sort."

"Orange blossom?" George asks.

"Yes! That's it." She takes another sip, finishing her sample.

"And you, sir," George says to me. "How did you find the whisky?"

"I'm not a fan." I set my glass down.

"Perhaps you'll like the single grain better."

"Brianna's the whisky drinker here," I say. "I'm more of a beer man."

"Then I hope you'll be able to sample the wide range of Scottish ales. Some of the finest."

"Why didn't you arrange a beer experience?" Brianna asks.

"Because I knew you'd enjoy this more."

She smiles at me, and in that moment, the peaty Scotch is the most delicious thing I've ever tasted, other than Brianna's pussy, of course.

I make it through the rest of the tasting with my tongue intact. Good thing, as I'll be putting it to use later. Once we leave, I turn to Brianna.

"I have another surprise for you," I say.

"Oh?"

"Yes. We leave tomorrow for Glasgow, as you know, but not until noon. Tonight we'll be dining together at the Dome."

"The Dome?"

"Yeah. I know how you Steels love to eat, so I asked the concierge where to take you for an elegant dinner that has a mix of Scottish and other cuisine."

"But Maddie..."

"I offered to let her tag along, but she insisted you and I go alone."

"She did?"

"Yeah." I squeeze Brianna around her waist. "I think she's accepting the two of us. She'll come around."

"I hope so. I hate that this bothers her so much."

"I do too, baby. We'll both take care of her."

* * *

According to the concierge at the Waldorf, the Dome restaurant in Edinburgh is known for its grand and opulent ambience, and it features luxurious decor that exudes elegance and sophistication. His words, not mine.

Brianna and I arrive at the historic building. Brianna's eyes go wide at the entrance's classic columns and grand doorway.

"Thinking of your sister again?" I ask.

"Yeah. For sure. She'd love all this architecture. She should really be here."

"She'll come someday." We walk into the restaurant and are greeted by the host.

But Brianna's eyes are still circles. The atrium is adorned with intricately designed columns, marble floors, and an eye-catching central dome with a stained-glass ceiling. Hence the name of the restaurant, I guess.

The host leads us to our table, and above us hangs a crystal chandelier. This is pure elegance...and I feel totally out of place.

Brianna Steel, though? She was born for elegance. She may be a cowgirl at heart, but she's just as much at home in a classy restaurant.

We choose to go with the chef's menu for the evening— smoked salmon with capers, red onion, and lemon; Scotch broth soup with lamb, barley, and vegetables; pan-seared duck breast with orange sauce, fondant potato, and wilted spinach; and Cranachan parfait with toasted oats and raspberries. Our waiter recommends a light Burgundy with dinner, and Brianna orders a Highland single malt when he asks for her cocktail preference.

I have a beer.

I'm done trying to be something I'm not. Scotch is for those nights when I'm pulling my hair out.

The food is all delicious, and we don't converse a lot during dinner.

When we arrive back at the hotel, we head to the bar for a nightcap.

Maddie is there, and seated with her is—

I groan. "You've got to be kidding me."

CHAPTER TWENTY-SIX

Brianna

I drop my mouth open and race toward Maddie's table. "Oh my God! Dave! What are you doing here?"

My cousin David Simpson, son of Aunt Marj and Uncle Bryce, rises with a smile on his handsome face, his blue eyes sparkling.

"Hey, Bree." He grabs me in a bear hug.

I pull back and echo my question. "What are you doing here?"

"I decided Brock and Donny couldn't have all the fun. I came to join the Rake-a-teers in the UK."

"Donny and Brock are no longer Rake-a-teers," I remind him. "And Donny's not even here."

"Yeah. Maddie just filled me in. I'm sorry to hear about Dragon."

Jesse hasn't said anything so far, but the tension is flowing off him in waves. He's behind me, and I can still feel his rigidity.

"Have you seen Brock yet?" I ask.

Dave shakes his head. "Nope. He and Rory had already retired when I got here. So I guess we're off to Glasgow tomorrow for a concert."

Finally Jesse speaks. "We know the schedule, Simpson."

Oh, God. Here we go again. I finally had Jesse in a happy

place, and now he's going to go all alpha on Dave for having the gall to actually sit and have a drink with his youngest sister.

Big brothers are a pain in the ass sometimes. I should know.

Dave moves to Jesse and holds out his hand. "Hey, Jess. I hear the tour has been a huge success so far."

Jesse takes Dave's hand, though I can feel his reluctance.

"Yeah," Jesse snorts out. "Except for the part where our drummer OD'd and we had to replace him."

"But he's okay," Dave, always the jovial optimist, says. "And I hear you got a killer replacement."

"That your cousin's paying for."

Dave ignores that comment, and I give him a subliminal thank-you.

Jesse, Jesse, Jesse... I thought you were lightening up.

Of course, it was the non-lightened Jesse I fell in love with, and nothing has changed. I'll love him for all time, despite what he thinks may happen.

"I guess congratulations are in order." Dave stays standing. "Why don't you two join us?"

It hasn't escaped my notice that Maddie hasn't said a word to me.

"Sure," I say.

Jesse says nothing, but he does hold out a chair for me. Dave finally sits back down after I'm seated. All the Steel men are gentlemen to a fault in a lady's company—even mothers, sisters, and cousins.

Jesse takes a seat.

"So you two are an item," Dave says again. "How'd Donny take that news?"

"He doesn't have a damned thing to say about it," Jesse

says. "He's marrying my sister."

"True enough. And Brock's got Rory. So that just leaves beautiful Maddie here..." He meets Maddie's gaze and smiles that gorgeous Dave Simpson smile.

Dave is widely considered the best-looking of all the male Steel cousins. He looks exactly like Aunt Marj—dark hair and fine features—but with Uncle Bryce's sparkling blue eyes.

Again, Jesse goes rigid.

But Maddie...

Maddie's got this gorgeous smile on her face—a smile I haven't seen since we were on the plane and she was basking in the pampering of our first-class seats.

Only this time, it's directed at a person, not a service.

And it's fuller and more radiant.

Surely she's not thinking...

Hell. Maybe she is. Both her sisters snagged a Steel. Why shouldn't she?

Why shouldn't she indeed?

Perhaps I can help it along.

"So what are the two of you doing?"

Dave nods to his beer on the table. "Having a drink."

"When did you get here?" I ask.

"About an hour ago. Flight was awesome, though I had a two-hour layover in London. But the first-class lounge was a great respite. I ate there, and I'm still full. When I arrived, I saw Maddie walking to the elevator, and she very sweetly agreed to have a cocktail with me."

"You call that a cocktail?" I glance at his beer and laugh.

"I call it a Scottish ale, lassie," Dave says in a really bad brogue, which makes Maddie erupt in laughter and Jesse give her an evil eye.

Old Jesse is back.

But that's okay. I love both Jesses. I love everything about each of them.

"So Mads..." I turn to my friend. "How was your evening?"

"Good. I had dinner with Brock and Rory, and they went straight up to their room afterward, but I decided to hang out down here for a while. I was just about to call it a night when Dave strode through the doors."

"How convenient," Jesse says dryly.

I resist an eye roll. I love the man, but really? They're having a drink. One drink.

On the other hand...Jesse and I fell for each other, and we didn't even have a date beforehand.

I've seen a certain chemistry between Maddie and Dave at Murphy's bar back home. Dave is a decent pool player, but he's the worst in our family. He's also a big flirt—he's one of the three original Rake-a-teers, of course—which is often why his pool game sucks. He's too busy charming the ladies, and Maddie's usually among them.

"Have you checked in to your room yet?" I ask.

"Yeah. I checked in online, dumped my bags there, and came right back down to meet Maddie."

"So they didn't lose your luggage." From Jesse.

Still a sore spot, even though it arrived the next day.

To be fair, the trip didn't start out great for Jesse. He was the only one of our party stuck in an uncomfortable coach seat. Not a big deal for some, but he's tall with superlong legs, so it must have been uncomfortable. Then the airline lost his luggage. It was still in Denver. He struggled with awful jet lag, but Rory got him through it, and their first concert was a massive success. But then Dragon got high with two groupies and wound up OD'ing. Jesse just found out today that Dragon won't be returning for the rest of the tour. He's going home and entering rehab.

So yeah... The trip had a rough start for Jesse.

But he and I are together now.

Of course, that's also bugging him because one, he thinks I'm too young to commit, and two, our career paths seem at odds.

I'm a romantic at heart. I think true love can conquer any conflict.

I guess we'll see.

As far as I'm concerned, Dave being here is a plus. He can hang with Maddie and give Jesse and me more alone time together.

She may be thinking the same thing, according to the radiant glow on her face and in her dark eyes.

I was hoping Jesse and I could go straight back to his room, but his rigid stance indicates he's not going anywhere until he sees his youngest sister safely to bed.

"So you came here," I say, "but we're leaving tomorrow to go to Glasgow."

Dave takes a sip of his beer and nods. "I know. I got the whole itinerary from Brock before you guys left. He wanted someone in the States to know where you were at all times in case of an emergency."

"Then who's the emergency contact now?" Jesse asks pointedly.

"It was going to be Dale." Dave takes another drink. "But when I tried to give him the info, he told me that he and Ashley were heading to London to hang with Donny and Callie. So I gave Henry and Brad all the info before I left."

"Great." Jesse gestures to a server. "I'm going to need a drink here."

We each had only two drinks at dinner—I had Scotch

and he had beer, and then we both had wine—so no harm in another.

The server comes quickly. "Yes, sir?"

"Bourbon, neat," Jesse says.

"Brand?"

"Surprise me."

She turns to me. "Ma'am?"

"Same, but I'll have the best you've got."

Jesse gives me an evil eye, but I ignore him. So I can afford good booze. Sue me.

"Bring him the same," Dave says. "It's all on me."

Jesse glares at Dave, but at least he doesn't say anything. How can he? Brock is paying for his substitute drummer. I know it sticks in his craw, but he'll soon see that the Steels are generous people who don't expect anything in return.

I hope so, anyway.

"So seriously," I say to my cousin. "What made you decide to come here?"

Dave drains the last of his beer. "I need some time off, Bree. I've been working with Dad and Uncle Joe nonstop since all the shit went down with the trafficking and then Wendy Madigan. Now that she's gone and we don't have any dark shadows hanging over us, I felt it was time to take a vacation."

I open my mouth, but he gestures me to stay quiet.

"I know, I know. Steels don't take vacations. Unless they finish college early and want to follow rockers around." He grins.

I give him a friendly swat.

"Anyway," Dave continues, "I've never seen Europe, and since Don and Brock are both here—"

"Donny's leaving after the UK portion," I remind him.

"Right. I know that. I found out when I talked to Dale.

Anyway, once Donny and Callie return to the States, I figured you and Brock might enjoy some company."

I jump up and hug him. "You mean you're staying for the whole tour?"

"Yup." He laughs. "I've got all my rooms booked in all the hotels, so I'm here for the duration."

"Isn't that great, Jesse? Maddie?"

Maddie's smile widens. Jesse's is nonexistent.

"I think it's wonderful," Maddie finally says. "The more the merrier."

Our drinks arrive, and I take a sip of the smooth bourbon. "Mmm. Delicious. What do you think, Jesse?"

After his sip, "Decent."

I can't help a laugh. "It's nearly as good as Peach Street, in my opinion."

He grunts.

Maddie finally turns to him. "Jess, what the hell is wrong with you? You had what I assume was an enjoyable dinner with Bree—"

"Dinner was perfect," he says.

"Right, so what's eating you?"

I know damned well what's eating him, and Maddie probably does as well. Why she's playing dumb is beyond me. But what can Jesse say? It's not like Dave said he came here to be with Maddie. He came because he needed a vacation—a well-earned one.

"Dragon," Jesse finally says.

Okay. Maybe I'm on the wrong track. He did just find out yesterday that Dragon's not coming back. Even though he has a replacement drummer who's more technically accurate than Dragon, Derek doesn't have that unnamed thing that makes Dragon's percussion shine.

If Dave's appearance were bothering Jesse, he'd say so. He's never one to mince words.

He downs his bourbon quickly and rises. "I'm hitting the sack."

I rise as well.

"No, Brianna. Stay here and talk with your cousin. I'm sure you have a lot of catching up to do."

"A lot of catching up?" I shake my head. "We've only been gone a week."

But Jesse doesn't reply. He simply throws a few five-pound notes on the table and leaves.

I take the money. "I'll return this to him."

"I see what's bothering him," Dave says. "Two of his sisters are engaged to Rake-a-teers, and he thinks I've come after the third one. Go with him. Tell him that's not what this is about."

"I will." I rise and glance at Maddie.

And that beaming smile that filled her whole face with beautiful light?

It's gone.

CHAPTER TWENTY-SEVEN

Jesse

Jesus fuck.

David Simpson? And Maddie? Seriously?

I breathe in deeply, trying to ease the tension that's turned my body into stone.

I made my peace with Brock and Rory.

I even made my peace with Donny and Callie, and I've gotten to the point where I'm glad I did. Holding on to a high school rivalry is ridiculous and immature.

I've made my peace—sort of—with Brianna's age, with the fact that she may not be able to commit to what I want to ask of her.

But Maddie? Really?

I have to let her go to a Steel too?

I laugh at the absurdity of my own thoughts. I don't want my littlest sister with a Steel, but *I'm* with a Steel.

Good going, Jess. You've become a hypocrite as well as an idiot.

I return to my room and close the door. Five minutes later, a loud knock.

I don't have to wonder who it is. I already know. I open the door to Brianna standing in the hallway. She doesn't look happy.

She walks right past me and then glares. "What the hell

was all that about?"

"He came here for one reason, and let's not pretend he didn't."

She whips her hands to her hips. "Then you'll be happy to know he told Maddie and me both, point-blank, to tell you not to worry. This is a vacation to him. A vacation with Brock, who he's the closest to of all our cousins. They're practically the same age."

"Bullshit. Did you see how he was looking at her?"

"That's just Dave. He's a flirt. He looks at all beautiful women that way."

"Not you."

"For Christ's sake, Jesse. I'm his cousin! Of course he wouldn't look at me that way."

"I know."

I'm being ridiculous, and I know it. What is it about the Steels that irks me so? Is it their money? Their privilege? Their generosity? The fact that two of my sisters fell in love with two of them?

The fact that I fell in love with one too?

Fuck it all.

I grab Brianna and kiss her.

Hard.

Hard, delving my tongue into her mouth and taking her with a kiss.

She responds, of course. I knew she would.

I lean into the kiss, until—

I rip my mouth from hers. "I can't. Not like this."

She touches her lips. "Like what?"

"I feel like I take you in anger a lot. That's not who I am, Brianna."

"I love who you are. If you need to lose yourself in me to

ease whatever you're feeling, I'm here for you."

I draw in a breath. "Do me a favor. Don't let me do that to you anymore. I'm a better man than that."

She smirks. "You're a wonderful man, Jesse. But truly, what is there to be angry about? Dave isn't here to woo Maddie, but what if he were? Would that be so terrible? Would it be the worst thing in the world for the Pike family to blend with the Steel family?"

I shake my head, shoving my fingers through my hair. "No. That's not it. That's not what I mean."

"Then what do you mean?"

"I mean... I don't fucking know. So much resentment has been tied up with your family for so long. It's not an easy thing to just let it go."

"I know." She touches my cheek.

God, I burn at her caress.

"Donny was the most difficult for you, but you got through that."

"Doesn't mean I still don't feel things."

"Of course you feel things. You've built up that resentment since you were eighteen."

"Younger than that," I admit. "It's hard to watch someone be as good as you when you know you've worked twice as hard."

She crosses her arms. "Now that's not fair. Donny worked as hard as anyone else on the football team. You know that."

I pull at my hair. "Damn it, that's not even what I mean. Your brother was an A-plus athlete, but so was I."

She pulls me to the bed, sits down, and pats the place beside her. "I think there's something you need to know about Donny."

"Trust me. I know all I need to know. I know he loves my sister. I believe it. I see the way he looks at her." I sigh. "It's the way I look at you, Brianna."

"Then let go of your resentment toward my family," she says. "Please. For me."

"I thought I had."

She kisses my shoulder. "Letting it go doesn't mean you turn it off like a faucet. Things will still creep up on you. That's the nature of harboring those feelings for so long."

"That sounds like it came straight from—"

"Aunt Melanie?" She laughs. "That's because it did."

"I was going to say a therapy session, but same difference."

"So accept that it'll still bug you from time to time, but recognize it for what it is, and tell yourself each time that you'll let it go. That it doesn't matter. Life isn't always fair, but that's not important. What's important is how you deal with that fairness or unfairness."

I can't help a smile then as I caress her soft hair. "Did you ever think of going into psychiatry?"

She laughs. "Are you kidding me? This cowgirl? I can't think of something that's more difficult to understand than the human psyche. I prefer my trees in the orchard. My horses in the barn."

"I'd say you have a knack for helping people."

She shakes her head. "I just repeat what I've heard Aunt Mel say since the day I could understand words. She's so brilliant. But she doesn't need me to be her protégé. That's Angie."

"Dave's sister?"

She clamps her hand over her mouth. "Shit. She told me that in confidence. She hasn't told her parents yet. Just Aunt Melanie and me."

"You certainly don't need to worry about me blabbing it," I say. "I doubt I'll say two words to Dave while he's here."

She swats me in the arm. "Oh yes, you will. We're all going to get along splendidly like one big happy family. Because, Jesse, we *are* family. Or we will be soon, whenever my brother and cousin get around to setting a date."

I can't help another laugh. "You sound just like Callie."

"Great." She rolls her eyes. "I don't want you thinking of me as your sister."

"Trust me," I say, narrowing my gaze. "I don't. But she gave both Donny and me that same speech about family and all the other bullshit. Even made us shake hands. I'm surprised she didn't make us hug."

"Maybe she should have. We Steels tend to be huggers. Except for Dale. He avoids touching people."

I pause a moment. "Why do you suppose that is?"

She twists her lips and looks away from me.

There's something you should know about Donny.

Her earlier words.

Donny and Dale were both adopted by the Steels when they were seven and ten, respectively. No one knows about their earlier lives.

Funny how I never considered that before. I was so hell-bent on envying and resenting the Steels for their good fortune, I never stopped to think that appearances can be deceiving.

"Fuck." I rub at my temples. "It's bad, isn't it?"

"It's not really my story to tell. I didn't even know about any of it until recently." She sighs. "But yeah, it's bad. I'll tell you if you'd like me to."

Fuck. All that rivalry with Donny Steel over him being chosen MVP over me, the quarterback. What happened to him and his brother? Abuse, most likely. Or neglect. Enough for the courts to terminate parental rights. Or maybe they were orphans, left alone by a tragic death of their parents.

"I'm sorry. Don't tell me. Not unless they say it's okay."

She nods. "It's probably better that way. It's in the past, and as you can see, both Dale and Donny are thriving now, thanks to our parents and the rest of the family. Aunt Mel especially. She got them through that first year, along with a child psychologist in Denver."

I gulp. Damn. "How can Dale and Donny be so different? Dale's such a recluse, and Donny was always the life of the party. He still is."

"People handle things differently. Some go inward, others outward."

"Melanie?"

I nod. "Yeah. Like I said, she's brilliant."

"She's Brock's mother."

She lets out a chuckle. "Well, of course she is. You know that."

"I do. It's just... I never thought about it before now. How Brock comes from a highly intelligent mom. His and Rory's kids could be that smart."

"My uncle Joe is no slouch either."

"I get that. But your aunt has written books, has helped people heal from trauma. She specializes in children, doesn't she?"

"She's retired now, but yeah, she did. She also saw adults, though. My father was her patient at one time." Her hand goes over her mouth once more. "Shit! What is wrong with me?"

"There's nothing wrong with you, Brianna." I throw my arm around her shoulders. "You trust me, and I trust you. If you want to tell me, I'll take whatever you say to my grave. And if you don't, that's okay too."

She caresses my arm. "I'd love to be able to confide in you

about everything. And I do trust you. But it's still all so new to me. My parents, aunts, and uncles kept so many secrets from us while we were growing up. You know one of the big ones."

"Your uncle Ryan and Wendy," I say. "Your new aunt."

"Yeah, but in my family's defense, they didn't know about Lauren and Jack or Pat Lamone. But the rest of it?" She sighs. "They knew."

And just like that, as if an angel swooped down from heaven, my burden about the Steels is lifted.

I'm in love with Brianna.

And her family, as rich as they are, are just as far from perfect as any other family. One day I'll ask her what happened to Dale and Donny—and why her father was in therapy—but not tonight.

Tonight, I'm going to enjoy no longer bearing such a heavy load in my head. I'm going to enjoy Brianna and not hold her family against her.

"I love you," I say.

"I love you too, Jesse."

"I'm no longer angry, so I want to make love to you. I want to love you the way you deserve."

CHAPTER TWENTY-EIGHT

Brianna

His words melt my heart.

Of course, my heart was already jelly from his love, from his kisses.

We undress each other slowly, and then he lays me on the bed, spreads my legs.

"So beautiful," he breathes. "Everything about you. Your pussy is glistening, Brianna."

"Only for you," I sigh.

My words are not an embellishment. I saved myself for a reason. Though I had other boyfriends and enjoyed experimenting, I never regretted not doing the actual act.

That was for Jesse only.

And now that he returns my love, I know I made the right choice.

Even if he didn't return it at first, it was still the right choice for me.

He hovers over me, trailing his lips over my cheek and then my neck and shoulders. "I'm going to taste every inch of you," he says. "Every fucking inch." He slides his lip over the top of my chest.

I close my eyes, sigh, arching my back. My skin is prickly all over yet warm, my flesh rosy, and between my legs, I'm already pulsing lightly.

Jesse stops at my breasts, squeezes them, swirls his tongue over one nipple.

I gasp. "God, feels so good."

"You have the most beautiful breasts, Brianna." He kisses one nipple and then the other. "I could spend all night on them alone. I could write a whole song about them. About how your nipples harden simply when I look at you, how your breasts are rosy and plump."

A soft sigh escapes my throat.

"But for now, I just want to suck on them, pinch them, tug on them. Make you feel it all the way down in your pussy."

"I do. I already feel it down there. I'm wet for you, Jesse. Wet and ready."

"I'm hard as a rock for you too, and I could take you now. But anticipation... I said I was going to taste every part of you, and I intend to."

He sucks on one nipple, twisting the other one between his fingers.

Sparks shoot through me, dancing around my body like a pinball before they end up straight in my pussy, right on my clit.

He spends a few more minutes on my breasts, but then he trails his lips downward, and he plants soft kisses on my belly, on the tops of my thighs.

"Please..." I gasp out when he avoids my pussy.

"We'll get there, baby."

My legs are spread, and he kisses and licks my inner thighs, which I know are wet from my juices. He slides down my legs, kissing the tops of my calves, and when he gets to one foot, he gives it a massage with his nimble fingers as he kisses each toe.

No one has ever paid attention to my feet like that before, and I like the feeling it evokes in me. Who knew that toes were an erogenous zone?

He continues with my other foot, massaging the instep as he kisses each toe, this time sucking them into his mouth.

When he's done with my feet, he travels back up, kissing my legs again, my inner thighs, and then spreading them farther open. My eyes are closed, and I'm entering a dream state...just waiting for him to slide his tongue over me, make me feel the way he did that first night when he took my virginity.

But seconds pass, and nothing happens. I open my eyes. Jesse is looking at me. Looking at me between my legs and pulling on his own shaft.

"I know a better place for that," I say.

"Just easing the ache a little, baby."

Then he lowers his head, and I ready myself. I ready myself for the invasion of his tongue and lips.

"God, you smell good." I hear him inhale. A deep breath. "And I know you taste even better."

He attacks then, not only with his tongue but with his lips and his teeth. He pulls at my pussy lips, making me insane. I don't know a woman alive who doesn't enjoy being eaten, and I'm no exception. Especially when Jesse Pike, my only love, is doing the job.

He moans and groans as he devours me, and I relish the sounds of his actions. The sucks, the slurps, and everything else. I lift my hips to give him better access, grind against his stubbly jawline.

He moves from my pussy lips up to my clit then, gives it a quick suck, and just as I am about to jump—

He flips me over quickly so I'm lying on my stomach. "Jesse, please... I need to come."

"Oh, you will... But I told you I was going to kiss every inch of you first."

The warmth of his body covers me, and his hard cock dangles between my butt cheeks. I lift my hips, searching for what I crave.

But then Jesse slides his lips over my shoulders, my arms, down to each hand where he kisses each finger, massaging my palms as he did my instep.

The sensation is so relaxing, yet my clit is throbbing, my pussy empty.

Being so relaxed and so horny at the same time... It's upsetting my equilibrium.

But Jesse clearly won't be rushed. He kisses and massages my other hand, going back up my arm, and then...his strong hands massage my shoulders.

"I love to touch you," he says. "Your skin is so soft, Brianna." He moves downward, massaging first my upper and then my lower back, and then his lips take over. He kisses my shoulder blades, down my spine, giving me shivers.

When he gets to my ass, he squeezes my butt cheeks, and then he swipes his tongue between the crease. A quake surges through me, as if I'm having a seismic reaction to his sliding his tongue over that forbidden place. I'll let him do whatever he wants to me. If he wants to fuck me there, I will let him. He already took one virginity. Why not the other?

"You taste so sweet," he grits out.

"Jesse... I'm aching for you."

"I'll give you what you need. What we both need."

But then he kisses the backs of my thighs, my calves, all

the way down to my feet, giving them another massage, and then sliding back up my body, his tongue leading the way.

Then his cockhead is between my ass cheeks. He wets it with my pussy juices and then slides it along the crease, nudging ever so lightly at my asshole.

"You can do it if you want," I say. "If you want to take me there, Jesse, I want you to."

He lowers himself so that his head is right at my ear. "You are a tempting little vixen," he whispers, "but you're not ready for that."

"I trust you."

"I know you do, and that means the world to me, Brianna. But there are things I need to do to you to prepare you for that. And right now...I just want to fuck you."

A second later, he's inside me, ramming into me from behind.

I'm still lying face down, my legs fully on the bed. And with each thrust, my clit rubs against the linens.

I begin climbing the peak, ready to skyrocket over it with Jesse by my side.

He thrusts, he thrusts, he thrusts... Going faster and then faster still. Easing that empty ache inside me, filling me as only he can.

One more thrust, and the friction hits my clit with a force so powerful I'm not sure I've ever come quite so hard. I soar off the precipice, embracing the euphoria, the nirvana.

"Jesse, come with me. Come with me please."

And with my words, he plunges into me once more, and with each contraction of his cock that I feel, I soar even higher.

Time seems to suspend itself as we travel together through the ecstasy of our climaxes. In my mind's eye, I see us holding hands, floating through the stars, our bodies in perfect synchrony.

In perfect harmony.

I'm not sure how much time has elapsed when he finally pulls out and rolls over onto his side.

"My God, you're amazing," he says.

I flip to my side as well and regard his handsome face. He's glistening with sweat, his hair pasted to his forehead and cheeks. "You're the amazing one. Thank you for that."

"My pleasure."

I yawn. "I'm so relaxed right now. Your kisses and those mini massages... It was all heaven, Jesse."

"Mmm," is all he says, closing his eyes.

I want to close mine as well. I want to sleep in bed next to him. It's something I've never done.

But I can't. I have Maddie to think of, and so does he.

"I guess I should go," I finally say.

He opens his eyes. "I know, baby. It won't always be like this."

I rise from the bed, go to the bathroom for a moment, and then return and put my clothes on. When I get back, Jesse has put his jeans on and pulled a T-shirt over his head.

"I'll see you to your room."

"You're so sweet. But it's just down the hallway."

He brushes his lips over mine. "Nonnegotiable." He opens his door. "Shall we?"

I walk out in front of him, look toward my room, nearly drop my jaw to the floor, and then push Jesse back into his room before he can see anything.

CHAPTER TWENTY-NINE

Jesse

"What the hell?" I ask.

"Jesse," Brianna says, "I just want to remind you what we talked about earlier. Tonight."

"Brianna, what's going on?"

"Remember, how you talked about you resenting my family...and how you're over it."

"Baby, get out of my way."

"Jesse, please—"

"Move, or I will move you."

She bites on her lips and steps out of the way. I walk outside the door and—

I race toward Brianna's room, because right outside the door...

Anger curls at the back of my neck. It's that crow pecking again. My youngest sister is in a clench, her mouth fused to David Simpson's.

I grab Simpson by the shoulders, pulling him off my sister and knocking him against the wall.

Maddie tumbles to the floor.

Then of course I'm stuck between a rock and a hard place. Do I pummel Dave Simpson? Or do I help my sister off the floor?

"For fuck's sake," I grit out.

I let Dave go and hold my arm out to Maddie, helping her up.

"Jesus, Jesse, what was that about?"

"He said he didn't come here for you," I say through clenched teeth. "That's what you said, right, Brianna? That's what you told me."

Dave smooths out his shirt from where Jesse grabbed it. "You've got a lot of nerve, Pike, when you were just in your room with my cousin."

"This is all ridiculous," Brianna says. "We're all adults here. But for God's sake, Dave, why didn't you tell me the truth?"

"I don't owe any of you any explanation," Dave says, keeping his voice steady. "But I was telling the truth. Neither Maddie nor I intended for anything to happen between us."

One look at my sister, though, and I'm pretty sure she got exactly what she wanted.

When the hell did she grow up?

I hold back a scoff. She grew up the same time Brianna did, and Brianna is all woman.

Brianna caresses my arm. "Everything's fine."

I draw in a deep breath. I let go of my envy and resentment of the Steels earlier. But when one shows up unexpectedly and I find him with his hands all over my baby sister...

My own hands are still clenched into fists, and everything inside me tells me to propel myself toward David Simpson and knock him to the ground, punch his smug little face in until it's unrecognizable.

But Brianna's right. Even Dave is right, though it drives me crazy. We are all adults here.

"Sorry," I say begrudgingly.

"No worries," Dave says, returning to his jovial self. "I'd probably have done the same thing if I saw you and Brianna in a clinch."

"She's not your sister," I say.

"Jesse," Brianna says, "it's the same thing in our family. We're a very close-knit group. All our cousins are like siblings to us."

"She's right," Dave says. "So I get what you're feeling. But it was just a kiss, man."

Maddie's face falls at his comment. She was hoping for more. Maybe she and I need to have a talk. I could get Brianna to talk to her, but Brianna's her same age, and I certainly didn't plan to fall in love so quickly and completely.

Brianna takes Maddie's arm. "Come on. We've got a big day tomorrow. You and I should go to bed."

Maddie doesn't smile, but she does give Dave a longing look before she goes with Brianna into the room, closing the door behind her.

"Just so you know," Dave says. "I don't use women."

That earns him my biggest scoff of the night. "You're one of the three Rake-a-teers," I say. "So I call bullshit."

"Was," he says. "And I don't know if you realize this, but the other two are engaged to your other two sisters."

"Don't remind me."

"Look." Dave holds his hands out in front of him. "I didn't come here looking to hook up with your sister. Maybe it will happen and maybe it won't, but it's not the reason. I was telling the truth when I said I needed a vacation. You don't know the half of what our family's been through."

I don't reply. How can I? He's right. I don't know a lot

of it. Brianna offered to tell me, but I could tell it made her uncomfortable.

"So..." Dave continues, "if you'll excuse me, I think I'll get some shut-eye." He begins to walk past me.

I grab his arm. "I got it. I get that you need a vacation. I get that you've had a hard time—that your family's had a hard time. I don't know the details, but I know it was bad. Harsh even. Probably heinous. But here's where we differ, Simpson." I stare him dead in the eye. "When my family falls on a hard time, we don't get a vacation. We can't afford it."

His gaze softens.

Which is not what I want.

I do not want, nor have I ever wanted, the Steels' pity.

Yeah, I've *really* let that resentment and envy go.

But as Brianna said, it will take time.

"What do you want me to say to that?" Dave finally asks. "Do you want me to apologize for having money? For being born into money? I won't. I had no control over that. I admit it's made my life a lot easier. And yeah, your life has probably been harder because you don't have money. Or at least not the kind of money we have. I sure as hell wouldn't expect you to apologize for that."

"No. I don't want you to apologize for it. But there are some things you'll never understand. Brianna, Donny, Brock... They'll never understand either, even though they're involved with my family."

"I get it, man. But I can guarantee you Brianna and I have seen and heard shit you don't even want to think about. Shit you probably can't even conceive."

I nod. "I understand. But David, two of my sisters are marrying into your family. Hell, I may marry into it myself someday. So if there's something we should know—"

He lifts his hand to cut me off. "All you need to know is that we're good and honorable people...despite what our ancestors may have done. We are not them."

"I got it. Good night."

Dave simply nods and walks down the hallway toward the elevators.

CHAPTER THIRTY

Brianna

I pounce on Maddie as soon as we get into the bedroom. "Okay, spill it."

Her cheeks are rosy, and her lips trembling. "I certainly wasn't expecting it. After all, he specifically said he had not come here for me."

"You asked me once if I had designs on your brother. I'm not proud of the fact that I lied to you, Maddie. But you know now that I've been in love with him for a long time, and miracle of all miracles, he seems to feel the same way. But I'm sorry I lied to you, and I'm asking you to be truthful with me now. Do you have designs on Dave?"

She draws in a breath and falls down on her bed. "I talk to Callie about it sometimes. How attractive I find him."

"He is a pretty boy, for sure," I say.

"That's what everyone says, but to me, he's so much more than a pretty boy. His smile takes my breath away, and those eyes..."

"I understand. I've always coveted my mom's blue eyes. They're so gorgeous."

"For God's sake, Brianna, you don't need to covet anything. Next to Rory, I'd put you as the most beautiful one in Snow Creek."

"I'm afraid I can't hold a candle to your sister. But thank you for the compliment. You and Callie are both beautiful too, each in your own way. I mean, come on. Your mother was a beauty queen."

Maddie rolls her eyes. "A beauty queen in local pageants, Bree. Your grandmother was a *supermodel*."

I'm not sure what to say to that. She's right, of course. I'm the granddaughter of supermodel Brooke Bailey, who was huge fifty years ago. But I never knew her because she and my mother didn't have the best relationship. She died long ago.

"I could tell you not to go falling in love with Dave," I say, "but who am I to say that? We Steels seem to have a habit of falling hard and falling fast."

"Don't worry," she says. "I'm not laboring under any delusion that the last of the Rake-a-teers is going to fall for me. But it would be nice to have someone to enjoy this trip with."

"That's what I'm for."

"I know, but it's different now." She looks down. "You're with Jesse. Everyone is paired off except for me."

"Cage and Jake aren't."

"Well, first of all, Cage is my cousin, so gross. And Jake has never done anything for me. Besides, they're both with the band."

"Jesse's with the band. So is Rory."

She sighs. "I know. But even though you can't spend as much time as you want with Jesse, and Brock can't spend as much time as he wants with Rory, you're still paired off. And as usual, I'm the odd one out."

"So that's what you want, then? You want Dave to be your *date* for the trip?"

"I certainly wouldn't be averse to it."

"Oh, Maddie," I say. "I don't want to destroy your dreams, but David just said earlier that he didn't come here for... You know."

"Yeah, I heard him. I was a little crestfallen when he said it, but you don't know what he said after you and Jesse left."

"I guess I don't. You want to enlighten me?"

"He just said he thought I was beautiful and he'd like to spend some time with me on the trip. He said what he did because he didn't want to piss Jesse off. But he also said he wasn't looking for anything serious. And he reiterated the fact that he didn't come here for me specifically. He came here because he needed a break but was glad I was here, and he asked if I'd like to spend time with him."

"To which you responded..."

"To which I responded...yes, of course, that I'd love to spend some time with him. Especially now that you and Jesse are together. It will give you some time to be alone with him and not feel like you have to be entertaining me."

"You already gave me that opportunity tonight when you let Jesse and me have dinner together."

"I know. I want to be fair to you and my brother. I don't want to be the lost lamb everyone has to be worrying about."

"That's not how we think of you, Mads."

She raises her eyebrows. "Isn't it, though? I suppose it's partially my fault. The way I told you all about how I felt so left out among you and the rest of the awesome foursome."

"I know, Mads. I'm so sorry about that. I honestly never knew."

"I know."

I think for a moment back to when I was in Maddie's room and noticed the quotes on her wall.

"I am an outsider looking in, absolutely." — David Bowie

"Why fit in when you were born to stand out?" — Dr. Seuss

"The worst part about feeling like you don't belong is trying to find a place to belong." — Trent Shelton

I should've noticed a lot sooner. But I hadn't been in Maddie's room for...a while, for sure. Over a year? Two years?

That's not being a friend.

"Please don't look at me like that, Brianna."

"Like what?"

"Like I'm the most pathetic creature on earth." She sighs. "So I'm feeling left out. So all my siblings are involved with Steels, and I'm the odd one out or the fifth wheel to the awesome foursome. I need to get over it. I need to be strong on my own two feet."

Again I think of her inspiring quotes. She's tried so hard to belong and never felt she did.

"After all," she continues, "no one can fix me but me. No one can fix my life but me. And I do want you to know how grateful I truly am for this trip."

"You could've come anyway. You didn't need me."

"But you've made it so amazing. Being able to fly in such luxury. I still feel bad that Jesse didn't get that."

"Don't you worry. He'll get it on the way home if I have to drag him into the first-class cabin myself."

"He'll come around. My brother may be bullheaded as... well...a bull, but he's not stupid. He'll eventually stop being so belligerent about accepting your help."

"Why did *you* accept my help, Maddie? I know your parents are very strict about not taking handouts. Not that what I gave you was a handout."

"You didn't make it feel like a handout. You made it feel

like it was a gift. A gift to a friend. And it made me want this trip more than ever because I felt like you and I could get closer." She sighs. "Until my brother fell in love with you, I guess."

I grab Maddie's hands. "I think we have gotten closer, Mads. I've enjoyed being with you, and I'm not going to stop being with you. Unless, of course, you want to be alone with Dave more often. But Jesse will still be in rehearsal and working with the band on other things a lot of the time while we're touring. You and I will still have lots of time to spend together."

"And Dave?"

"Dave can hang out with Brock. Or you can hang out with Dave, and I can hang out with Brock. You and I will definitely have some girl time. I swear it, okay?"

She pulls me into a brief hug. "I'd really like that, Bree. This has been an amazing trip so far, and honestly, I'm really glad Jesse broke up that thing with Zane."

"I am too," I say, "especially after what happened with Dragon."

"Do you think Zane would have given us drugs?"

"No. I have no reason to believe he even does drugs. But it just wasn't a good idea. We both thought it was for our own reasons."

"Why did you want it?" she asks.

"Because your brother had basically told me whatever had been between us was over. That he had to keep his mind on the tour. He was right, of course. So I just decided, why not have a little fun? Zane is attractive and seemed like a decent guy. If a decent guy takes two consenting women back to his room, that's his business. It's what rockers do. Jett probably did it before he met Heather."

"I suppose you want to know why I wanted it as well."

"I just assumed it was for the same reason, Mads. You wanted to have a little fun. And Zane Michaels is hot. And he's famous. A huge rock star."

She bites her lower lip. "That's part of it, for sure. But there's more of a reason."

"You want to tell me?"

"It made me feel...beautiful."

I cock my head. "Maddie, you *are* beautiful. My God. How can you not see that?"

"I see it. But I've watched both my sisters snag Steels. And I've seen how men hang all over you guys—you, Sage, Angie, and Gina—at school and even at home. At Murphy's."

"You've always gotten your fair share of attention from men," I say.

"Have I, though?"

"Yeah, Maddie. You have. Are you truly the only one who doesn't see it?"

She sighs. "I've been thinking about talking to your aunt."

"Melanie?"

"Yeah. Do you think she would talk to me?"

"I know she would, but I don't think you need therapy, Maddie. You just need to look at yourself in the mirror and stop comparing yourself to your sisters—and to my cousins and me."

"You make it sound so simple."

"That's because it *is* simple. But if you think talking to someone would help, absolutely, talk to Melanie. She's amazing. I could arrange for her to see you virtually while we're here."

"Ugh. No. I hate that idea. I'd rather see someone in

person."

"Then the only problem is that we're about to go to Glasgow, and then we're going to be on the European continent for the next couple of months. And you probably want an English-speaking therapist."

That gets a laugh out of her. "Yeah, I guess that would be good."

I grab a pillow and throw it at her. "I promise to talk to Melanie for you when we get home, or you can certainly find someone else."

"In Snow Creek?"

"You'll have to go to Grand Junction. Or you can do it online. But Aunt Melanie will be able to refer you to someone perfect for whatever you need."

"What will I do until then?"

I bop her with the pillow again. "You start believing in yourself, Maddie. You start looking in the mirror and seeing yourself as other people see you. Beautiful and brilliant and a sweet, good friend. A person who has empathy, who feels things. And if my cousins and I have failed to realize that, then that's on us, not you."

"I'm probably not being fair. You've always tried to include me."

"Of course we have. But as I've said before, we just may not think about it as much as we should because we're all family, and we're always together. Our family is very close-knit."

She rolls her eyes. "You think?" This time she pops me with a pillow.

I grab another and pop her back. She grabs it from me and chases me around the hotel room until I pounce on my bed, grab my original pillow, and bean her over the head.

HARMONY

We both collapse onto our beds, laughing.
And I sleep soundly through the night.

CHAPTER THIRTY-ONE

Jesse

The train trip to Glasgow is short and uneventful, and once we get to our hotel—this one isn't as fancy as the ones in London and Edinburgh—we check in quickly, and then the band and I head straight to the venue for rehearsal and soundcheck.

After that, we catch a light dinner together.

I don't see Brianna at all after checking in to the hotel. I don't know if she's going sightseeing today, but I'll go out with her tomorrow morning before we head back to London for the encore concert.

"Your jaw's clenched, Jesse," Rory says.

"How can it be clenched?" I tear a piece of roll with my teeth. "I'm eating."

"Let it go. I know you're bothered about Dave being here."

"I'm not."

"Oh, please." Rory shakes her head. "We may be four years apart in age, Jesse, but I know you better than you know yourself."

"I mean it, Ror. I've made my peace with it."

It's not lying, exactly. I don't like the idea of anyone in my little sister's pants. I wasn't thrilled about it with Callie and Rory, for that matter. But Maddie...

"She's so young," Rory says, as if reading my mind.

"Yeah, she is."

"Same age as...Brianna."

"Yeah, I was waiting for you to bring that up."

"So get over yourself. The Steels are good people. I can vouch for them."

"You can vouch for Brock."

She shakes her head and swallows the bite of roll she took. "I can vouch for all of them," she says. "Callie and I have done a lot of talking about the family, and we've gotten to know them well. I mean, we already knew them, but since we got involved with members of their family, we talk to them more. Spend more time with them. They're good people, Jess. But I think you already knew that."

"I did." I take a sip of water.

"And for what it's worth, I agree about Maddie. She's very young. But so is Brianna, and she seems to know what she wants."

"Yeah... I worry about that a bit."

"Why?"

This isn't stuff I really talk to my sister about, but I need to confide in someone. Cage and Jake left our dinner early, so Rory and I are alone.

"It's hard to put into words, Ror. I'm not the kind of guy who wears his feelings on this sleeve."

"Except you *are*, Jess. You're an artist. You write songs about the feelings you're having."

"I've never written a song about this," I say, "and that's the God's honest truth."

"What are you getting at?"

I sigh. "I've never told a soul this. Except for Brianna, of course, but I'm not sure she understands."

"Go on."

"I've been attracted to her for a while now. In fact, we even shared a kiss before we left for the tour."

Rory's eyes pop open wide. "You *did*?"

"Yeah, outside of Murphy's one night. She's so beautiful, but I know a lot of beautiful women. Hell, I grew up surrounded by beautiful women."

"Moms and sisters don't count."

"I know that. But it's not like I'm mesmerized by beauty or anything. I've seen beauty before. I've been with beauty before. I've fallen in love with someone beautiful before. But with Brianna, it was just..."

"Quick?" she asks.

I scratch my chin, thinking. "Not quick so much as... unexpected. And different. Very, very different."

"So, not quick..."

"Yeah, not quick after all. Because when I'm honest with myself, I realize that I've been noticing her for the last several years. And there are things about her that I respect so much. Like her devotion to her family and to her ranch. I mean, other than Brock, who else is that devoted to the ranch?"

"Dale," she says.

"He's not devoted to the ranch so much as to wine. The art of making wine."

"But I think it's the same thing," Rory says. "He's staying home, working the land. Taking part in the family business. Whereas most of them aren't."

"What does Dave even do?"

"To be honest, I have no clue." She chuckles. "I guess we should ask."

"I think Brianna said he works with his dad. So I suppose

he does contribute to the family business, though he's not working the land."

"I think you're right, come to think of it."

"But Brianna's different," I say. "It's like the land is part of her. She looks the part. All cowgirl. A hundred percent. None of the rest of them are like that."

"Excuse me?"

"Except for Brock, of course."

"But you don't think of Brock that way."

"Not even a little bit. I'm sure he's a very handsome man, sis, but unlike you, I'm only attracted to one sex."

She laughs a little then. "It's funny. I really had no clue whether I'd end up with a man or a woman, and when Brock came along and pursued me, my first inclination was that he'd be a great father for my child."

"What?" I clench my jaw.

"Yeah. I actually asked if he'd be willing to father a child for me."

"You *what*?"

"I did. Not my finest moment, of course. But after Raine and I broke up, I realized what I really wanted was a child."

"And he said what?"

"He refused. So I went to a sperm bank."

"You *what*?" I echo myself.

"Yeah. But the counselor I talked to didn't think I was ready after we went through all the questions."

"And *are* you?"

"I am, Jesse. But Brock and I have decided to wait a few years. Because if the band takes off, I don't want to be going on maternity leave just yet."

I'm not sure what to say to that. Because, yeah, the band

may indeed take off. And if it does, we need Rory. But she could still tour. Up until probably five or six months. Then once she had the kid, she could come along. But Brock would have to come with her, or she'd have to bring a nanny for the baby. Of course, being married to Brock Steel, she'll be able to afford the best nanny in the business. Maybe she wants to take a more hands-on approach to motherhood. Knowing Rory, I'd bet everything that's it.

Rory and Brock have the same problem Brianna and I do. He's dedicated to working on the ranch. Of course, they fell in love before we knew the band would be going on tour. Before Rory had even officially joined the band. I'll talk to her about how they plan to handle it, but some other time.

"That's your decision," I say.

"Of course, I'm almost twenty-nine years old," she says. "We probably shouldn't wait too long."

"Are you kidding me? Women are having babies in their thirties now, even in their forties. You've got plenty of time."

"That's what Brock says too."

"But you want a child. You want to be a mother."

I can see it in her eyes as she gushes. "Absolutely, Jess. It's the thing I've always wanted most since I was a little girl. Don't you want kids?"

I have to stop and think about that. Kids aren't something that have ever popped onto my radar, but for Brianna to have my baby...

Damn.

My dick is getting hard just thinking about it.

Planting my seed in her, watching it grow. Then having a little boy or girl who's half Brianna and half me. Dark hair and dark eyes, of course, because that's what we have. And blessed with Brianna's beauty.

"I think I do."

"You think?"

"Maybe it's a difference between men and women, or maybe it's just the difference between me and you, Ror. But I honestly haven't given it a thought. But yeah, now that I've let the thought sink in, I *do* want kids. With the right woman."

"And you've found her?"

"I'd like to think I have. But that's what this conversation was originally about. How my love for her is so different from any other love I've felt. It's raw, almost animalistic sometimes. Yet it's sweet and pure the next minute. It's like she completes me, and I know that sounds cliché." I gaze out the window of the restaurant, taking in the Scottish landscape. "I can't even describe what I mean by it, because those words aren't even strong enough."

Rory chuckles and shakes her head. "You really are in love, Jesse."

"I am, and what concerns me is that she's so young, and she's been pining after me for so long, so is she really feeling what I'm feeling? Or is this just infatuation come to life?"

"I don't know."

Disappointment flickers through me. But honestly, what was I expecting? For Rory to say, *Oh, of course, Jesse. She's absolutely that in love with you. I can see it on her face.* Because the truth is, that's not a kind of love you can see on someone's face. I can look at Brianna with all the love in my eyes, but I've looked at other women that way as well. No, this is something that's inside, visceral, part of me.

"I appreciate your honesty," I say. "Because I just don't know either."

CHAPTER THIRTY-TWO

B r i a n n a

After the concert, Maddie and I, along with Brock and Dave, head backstage. Tomorrow, Jesse and I get to explore Glasgow together in the morning, but in the afternoon, we'll take the train back to London, have the encore concert the next evening, and then board a late flight to Paris.

Paris...

Again I think of my sister, Diana, who would love being here to see all the old architecture. But I'm taking lots of photos for her. And she's probably already studied all these buildings in her classes.

Zane Michaels stays away from us again, which is fine by me, and apparently fine by Maddie as well, as she and Dave are holding hands.

Brock takes me aside. "What do you make of that?"

"What do *you* make of it? You're closer to Dave than I am."

"Yeah, but you're closer to Maddie."

"Did Dave say anything to you?"

Brock shakes his head. "Nope. But we're guys. We don't talk about that shit."

"You mean you never told Dave about any of your antics with Rory?"

"Not really. We talked generally about it, but I don't kiss

and tell...anymore."

I give him a swat on his arm. "Yeah, I know you Rake-a-teers."

"Hey, Dave and I were just always trying to keep up with your brother."

"He's a little older than you are."

"I'm serious. Dave and I tried so hard. We even had a threesome back at school."

My jaw drops. "TMI, Brock. TMI."

My cousin's cheeks burn red. "Shit, I can't believe that just slipped out. I didn't mean to say that to you, Brianna. You know, you being a girl and all."

"Woman," I correct him. "How on earth did you get mixed up in something like that?"

"I told you. I don't kiss and tell. Suffice it to say that once was enough for both of us. Seeing each other naked was kind of weird."

"God, I bet. That's gross."

Though I nearly did the same thing with Maddie only a few nights ago. I even thought about how I would feel seeing Maddie naked. I figured if she and I didn't touch each other, maybe it would be okay. But I know how much men like girl-on-girl action, and I bet Zane was after that. Good thing that got broken up.

"So what are you guys doing tomorrow morning?" I ask.

"Well... Rory and I are joining you and Jesse on your tour."

"Oh." I force a smile. "How nice."

"It's a tour, Brianna. A guided tour. It's not like you're going to, you know, have any alone time."

"I know. You're right."

"I'm pretty sure Dave and Maddie are coming too."

"The more the merrier," I say, hoping to sound excited.

Brock is right, of course. It's not like Jesse and I would be alone on a guided tour. We'll probably catch lunch with the other four and then grab our stuff from the hotel and hit the train station.

"Rory and Jesse were amazing tonight," I say.

"They were," Brock agrees. "I think this is the best they've sounded together since we got here."

I smile at that, wondering if I had anything to do with it. Because when Jesse sings love ballads, I swear to God he's singing straight to me.

They only sang one ballad. The rest of the numbers were pure rock and roll.

But even then, I imagine he's singing to me. I feel him. I feel him in me, in my heart and my soul, and as his voice carries straight to my ears, he's inside me, a part of me.

Jesse and Rory are talking to fans.

Eventually they make their way over to Brock and me.

"You were so amazing." I grab Jesse in a hug. "Brock and I were just talking about how we've never heard you and Rory sound better than you did tonight."

He kisses my cheek. "Yeah, we were totally in sync tonight. It's like we were anticipating each other in a way we never have before."

"Whatever it was, it was awesome," I say.

Dave and Maddie approach us.

"Jess, you rocked it," Dave says.

Jesse, somewhat reluctantly, takes Dave's hand. "Thanks."

I nod at him. "He has a name."

"Dave," he says.

Dave cocks his head. "Hey, cool. I don't think I've ever

heard you call me Dave before. It's always Simpson."

"Okay, Simpson."

Dave, jovial as ever, simply laughs it off. "Awesome job, Pike. You rocked it." Then he turns back to Maddie.

Jesse is staring, and not nicely.

"You going to make your peace with that?" I ask.

"Do I have a choice?"

"Nope." I grab his hand. "Come on. I want to talk to Rory."

Brock and Rory are only a few steps away. "Rory," I say, "you were the best I've ever heard you. You and Jesse both."

She grabs me and hugs me. "Thanks so much, Brianna. We really were rocking tonight. I'm not exactly sure why."

"Maybe the talk we had before the concert," Jesse says.

"Yeah, maybe."

"Talk about what?" I can't help asking.

"Music, mostly," Jesse says.

I have an inkling he's not telling me the whole truth, but I'm not going to push it because I have everything I want. Jesse rocked it tonight. He's amazing, and he loves me.

A few more groupies come up to Jesse, but he holds tight to my hand, making it clear that we're together.

It warms me inside, keeps a smile on my face. I'm sure I look like an idiot, but I don't care.

When the crowd finally dies down, Jesse and I head for the limo alone.

When we get back to the hotel, Jesse walks me not to his door but to mine.

"You don't want to..."

"Oh, hell yes, I do." He grabs my hand and leads it to the bulge in his crotch. "I want you so much. My adrenaline is still flowing, and I need you."

"Let's go to your room."

"I was just thinking that if you're in your room, Maddie will have more of a desire to stay there."

"Look, whatever this is between Maddie and Dave, it just started. He's not going to take her to bed the first night."

Jesse stares at me, glaring. And I know exactly what he's thinking.

"Jesse... It's different."

"Just how is it different? First of all, this is the second night Dave's been here, and you and I ended up going to bed together the first night we were in London. The first night, Bree."

"You know what?" I huff. "So what if it does happen? She's a grown woman, Jesse. She's my age. My fucking age. And Dave is a good guy."

Jesse breathes in, lets it out slowly. "Do you have any idea how much I want you right now?"

"Since my hand is still on your dick, yeah, I have a pretty good idea."

"Just when I think I'm getting over everything. Oh, what the fuck?"

Then he leads me toward his room, opens the door, and we walk inside.

I expect him to grab me and kiss me hard. It's what usually happens as soon as we get into his room, but this time he doesn't.

"You okay?" I ask.

He closes his eyes. "Yeah."

"Oh my God, stop picturing it."

He snaps his eyes back open. "I'm not picturing it. Not the act itself, anyway. If I do that, I'll wait outside your cousin's room and punch him into next week."

"Then stop thinking about it. Stop letting it drive you crazy. You think Donny liked it any better when you took me to bed?"

"Brianna..."

"Besides, we don't even know if it will happen. It probably won't."

Except Jesse's right. *We* did it the first night, and that was before we had so much as held hands. Dave and Maddie were holding hands all night.

"Would you like it better if you knew for sure one way or the other?"

"God..." He rakes his hands through his hair. "No."

"Good. Now stop ruminating on it and take me to bed, Jesse. Take me to bed, forget all your troubles, and lose yourself inside my body."

In a flash his mouth is on mine, his tongue devouring me.

He's always so hot and needy after a concert. As if his adrenaline is still on high and he needs to get it out.

I will always be his willing vessel.

He breaks the kiss quickly. "I want... I want to rip your clothes off," he says through gritted teeth. "I want to rip that tank top right off your body."

"It's a Dragonlock tank top," I say.

"That's right, Bree. I want to rip right through the word *dragon*. Tear it from your chest."

As much as I'd love for Jesse to do that to me, I love this tank top. I don't want it in shreds. I can get another one just like it, but I've had this one for several years. It's what I always wore when I was thinking of Jesse. Worshiping from afar.

So I fling it over my head myself and toss it on the floor.

"Now the bra," he growls.

I remove it quickly, tossing it on top of the tank. My breasts fall gently against my chest.

Jesse sucks in a breath. "How the hell can you be so fucking beautiful?"

I don't think he wants me to answer. Any answer I could give would make me sound conceited, and that's not how I'm feeling. That's not how I've ever felt. I simply nibble on my lower lip, waiting for him to tell me again what to do.

"Fuck, you're sexy." He stares at me. Glares at me. Devours me with his eyes. "Everything about you, Brianna. Your beautiful dark hair, your mesmerizing eyes with those fucking long lashes. Your pink cheeks, your beautiful red puckered mouth. Your tiny ears, slender neck. Your shapely shoulders. And those tits. Perfectly round and full, with nipples not too small and not too big. Perfection. Even the color. Brownish pink. Darker than most. Darker than I expected with your skin tone. You're fucking perfect, Brianna, as if you were carved by an artist."

I swallow, my flesh heating.

"I never dreamed you would feel this way about me," I say.

"I never wanted to," he admits. "At least I never *thought* I wanted to. I can't fight it any longer, Brianna. I don't *want* to fight it anymore."

"And I don't want you to."

"Take off the rest of your clothes," he snarls.

Perhaps I should stop wearing cowboy boots. If I were wearing flip-flops, I could have them off in a millisecond, but boots? They take a while longer. I have to sit down and pull off each boot, and then my socks. Once they're gone, I shed my jeans easily, and soon I'm standing in nothing but a black lace thong.

Jesse draws in a breath, closing his eyes and then opening

them. "You have the firmest, plumpest ass. I want to rip that thong from you."

"Do it," I say.

And I want him to. I don't care about this thong. I don't care about any thongs. I don't even like thongs, but I wear them because I hate panty lines more than I hate the feeling of a thong riding up my ass.

He slides his fingers beneath my waistband and gives the thong a good yank.

And then it's gone, the lace between his fingers, and I hardly felt it.

He looks at me then. Rakes his gaze from the top of my head to my toes.

"So fucking perfect. Your beautiful hair, your intense dark eyes. Those lashes—I've never seen lashes quite so long, Brianna. Your rosy cheeks, and your perfectly shaped full lips. And that pussy. The most beautiful and dazzling pussy I've ever seen in my life."

I gasp, his words trailing over me like slick syrup.

"And those long and shapely legs wrapped around me as they were meant to."

My flesh is on fire, and it's culminating between my legs. If I don't get him inside me soon, I may combust.

"Sit on the bed, Brianna."

I walk the few steps to the bed and obey.

He stalks toward me, his eyes on fire. "I'm going to unclasp this beautiful belt buckle from you, and then I'm going to slide my jeans over my hips, and bring out my cock. I'm going to force it between your lips, Brianna. And I'm going to fuck your mouth."

My heart goes into double time. He's so beautiful, and

as I watch him, his shirt still on, unbuckle the gorgeous brass belt buckle I gave him, and then free his cock, I'm mesmerized. Completely and totally mesmerized.

He brings it forward, holding it at its shaft. He's already hard, and I take a moment to look at him. At the skin a shade darker than the rest of him, at the vein that twirls through it like a meandering river. At his balls, already scrunched toward his body. And at his muscular thighs, dusted with dark hair.

He's magnificent.

Majestic.

One more step, and the head of his cock nudges against my lips.

I open for him willingly, and he slides it inside slowly.

He's huge, and try as I might, I can't take all of him. I give it a good college try, and I take three-quarters of him.

He closes his eyes and groans. "Fuck..."

I want to tell him how much I love doing this for him, how much it means to me that he'll let me. But my mouth is full at the moment, and I have no intention of letting go.

I slide my mouth over him again, taking him slightly farther this time. Then I bring my right fist around his shaft and pull up as I bring my mouth over all the way to the head. Now lubricated with my saliva, my hand helps me take all of him, and I slide back over until his head hits the back of my throat. I hold myself in check, getting used to the invasion, as he groans above me.

"God, yes," he groans. "Take me. Take all of me. Take all of me into your sweet mouth."

CHAPTER THIRTY-THREE

Jesse

She's amazing. It's not the best blow job I've ever had, but it's the most perfect. It's the most perfect because of how into it *she* is. She wants to please me, and in turn, I want to please *her*.

So as much as it pains me to do so, I withdraw.

She lifts her eyebrows. "Jesse?"

"If you keep doing that, I'll come so quickly. I don't want to come yet, Brianna. I don't want to come until you've come. I don't want to come until you've come twice, maybe three times."

"That doesn't seem fair."

"Trust me. It's fair. Do you know how turned on I get when you come?"

She trembles but doesn't reply.

"When you come, Brianna, I feel it. I feel every contraction of your pussy. I feel every shiver that goes through your body. I feel every fragment of ecstasy that crawls across your nerves. I feel it."

"You...do?"

I do. I'm not lying to her. I feel what she feels.

"I do," I say.

"My God... As if I couldn't love you more..."

"You only need to love me the way you love me," I say.

"Love is love, Brianna."

"But it's not, Jesse. What I feel for you is..." She stops.

"You don't have to try to explain it. I sure can't explain what I feel for you. I don't think there are words."

"Jesse, I know you think I may not feel what you're feeling. I know that's your fear." She caresses my face. "But I want to alleviate those fears. There's only one man for me. There will only ever be one man for me."

God, I hope she's right. I hope she knows it in her heart and soul. But damn. When I was twenty-two, I didn't know which end was up.

I sit next to her, my dick still hard, but this talk is probably more important than anything.

"I don't want to push you, Brianna."

"Are you kidding me? I'm the one who's been pushing you."

Her remark makes me chuckle. "At first, yeah. You absolutely were. I thought of you as a young kid who couldn't possibly know what she wanted. But somewhere along the way, I realized I was keeping myself from feeling what I wanted to feel. So I let it out. And it's... It's indescribable, Brianna. Fucking indescribable. It's like you are me."

"But Jesse, that's how I feel too."

I cup her cheek, kiss her lips gently. Do I fight her on that? Do I just let her think what she thinks?

I choose to let it be.

Because there's a good chance she really *does* feel for me what I feel for her. And if she doesn't? Well, my heart will be broken eventually. I can't allow myself to think about that right now. Not when we're heading back to London tomorrow for our UK farewell concert.

"I believe you, baby. I believe we love each other very much."

"But..."

"But nothing."

I could talk about how our careers are at odds, about how she's so much younger and may not actually know what she's feeling yet.

But she's not me. I choose to embrace this moment. To rise, shed the rest of my clothes, lie down with her on the bed.

Our lovemaking is usually so frantic, but right now I just want to sink inside her—sink inside her and make love to her slowly.

Show her my love rather than my ache and my need.

I pull her into my arms so that we're facing each other side to side. Then I slide her thigh over my hips, position myself at her entrance, and glide inside.

She melts against me, glides with me, as I pull out and thrust back in.

We move together, and we become perfect harmony, just gazing into each other's eyes, as I slide in and out of her.

The feeling is so intense, as if my whole body is inside her, being loved by her sweetness and sexiness. As if I'm held by her heart as well as her body.

We continue to make love slowly, whispering sweet nothings to each other.

I love you, Brianna.

I love you, Jesse.

You're everything to me.

You're all I ever wanted.

We're surrounded in a cloud—a cloud of love and lust and pleasure and passion. Of completion.

We stay that way for moments, timeless moments, as I slide in and out of her body, as she gives herself to me and I to her.

And then, when I feel the contractions of her pussy, her quick intake of breath, signaling her climax—

I slide inside harshly, releasing. Releasing everything into Brianna. Everything I am and will be, I give to this woman.

And I know...

I know that whether this works out for the long term or not...

I will *never* love this way again.

★ ★ ★

When I wake up, the lights are still on. Brianna is still facing me, her eyes closed. My dick has gone flaccid and has slid out of her, but the perfection of the moment isn't lost. I gently lay her down on her back, and then I check the time.

The middle of the night. Two a.m.

Brianna was supposed to go back to her room.

I don't want to disturb her, so I place her under the covers and kiss her forehead. Then I slide my jeans back on to go check on Maddie.

I find Brianna's purse and grab her key card. That way I don't have to wake Maddie up by knocking. I take both my key card and Brianna's and leave my room, walking the few doors to hers.

For a moment I stand there.

Do I want to do this? Do I want to check up on my little sister?

What if I find David Simpson in there? What will I do?

"Fuck it," I say, sliding the key above the reader and then opening the door softly.

I walk in as quietly as I can, and then I sigh in relief.

My sister lies asleep, alone, in her bed.

I walk back, ready to leave, when—

"Who's there?"

I turn. Maddie is sitting up in bed, squinting her eyes.

"It's just me, Mads."

"Jesse?"

"Yeah. Sorry to wake you. I just wanted to check up on you and make sure you're okay because Brianna and I fell asleep. She meant to come back here."

Maddie looks around nervously, darting her gaze back and forth.

"Oh. That's sweet of you, Jesse, but as you can see, I'm just fine. Go back to Brianna. Enjoy your time together."

I nod. "Okay."

I turn, but then I notice something strange.

A sliver of light under the bathroom door that I didn't see before.

My heart drops into my gut as the door opens.

"Oh my fucking God," I say, averting my eyes.

David Simpson, naked as a damned baby.

My body tenses, and I feel like a bucket of freezing cold water has been drenched over my head.

I thought I was prepared for this.

But when I saw Maddie alone, I let my guard down.

"Shit." Dave returns to the bathroom and comes out a few seconds later with one of the white plush ropes wrapped around himself.

"What the hell are you doing here, Pike?"

"Checking on my sister, thank you very much."

"After you got done fucking my cousin?" Dave says.

With everything in me, I want to pummel him into next week. I could do it to that pretty boy.

I draw in a breath, hold it a few seconds, exhale.

Fuck. Didn't help.

"Jesse—" Maddie begins.

"Shut up," I say to her, and then I turn to Dave. "Just so I don't have to say it again, you shut up too."

He chuckles, shaking his head. "You've got some nerve."

"Did you not hear me? I said shut up."

Dave crosses his arms, looking like a diva in that robe. "And in what world do I have to answer to you?"

"In the world where you're fucking my sister, you jackass."

"Right. That same world where you just fucked my cousin."

"She's not your sister," I say through gritted teeth.

"What if she were? What if it was Angie or Sage instead of Brianna? You think that makes one bit of difference to me?"

"I don't care. We're not having this conversation." I motion to Maddie. "Get dressed. You'll stay with Brianna and me tonight."

"I will not," Maddie says. "I'm the same age Brianna is. Older, in fact, by a month or so. You already broke up my shot with Zane Michaels."

"He's a player. And so is Dave Simpson."

"No more than Donny or Brock are. And they settled down... With our sisters, Jesse."

Interesting. The look I'm getting from David Simpson right now tells me all I need to know. He doesn't have any intention of settling down with my sister. He's fucking her, plain and simple.

"Go back to Brianna, Jesse," Maddie says.

I've got to get a handle on this.

What David is doing with Maddie is no different from what I'm doing with Brianna. Except that I have feelings for her, and I did the whole time, even though I refused to admit it to myself.

And for all their other faults, Donny and Brock both have serious feelings for my other two sisters. But David Simpson is just getting his rocks off.

And Maddie is better than that.

"You're a lying son of a bitch," I say to Dave.

Dave steps toward me, puffing out his chest, which really doesn't work in that robe. "We've been through this before. I needed a vacation. I didn't come here to seduce your sister. This?" He gestures to Maddie. "It just happened. And for God's sake, Pike. Your sister's a beautiful woman. I've known her for a long time."

"Are you going to take her on a date?"

"From what I hear, you didn't take Brianna on a date."

God, he's right, and I hate it. I'm just so fucking mad. So fucking mad at the Steels. All the resentment I've carried inside me for so long—all the resentment I swore to Brianna I was letting go. Every time I think I'm done dealing with it, it creeps back to me.

"He's right," Maddie says, "and you know it."

Yeah, I know it. Doesn't make it any easier to bear. Doesn't make any of this any easier.

Then I realize something.

I was attracted to Brianna Steel. I've been attracted to her for a long time. I just kept myself in check, didn't let those feelings grow, and not just because she was ten years my junior.

No. Because she was a Steel.

Then my two sisters had to fall for Steels.

And I started looking at Brianna a bit differently.

Falling into bed with her that first time was no accident. In retrospect, I had been hoping for it to happen.

I draw in one more breath, and this time I count to ten silently.

A little bit of tension fades from my body—but only a little bit.

This will take time. I can say the words I want to say. I can say that I'm over my resentment of the Steels, and I can even truly believe that.

But the feelings? These feelings I've harbored for almost all my thirty-two years? They will take a little while longer.

"What are your intentions?" I ask David.

"I don't have to answer that."

"I think you just did." I gaze at my sister. "I'll leave you now. I'll accept that you're an adult and that you can do what you want. But you deserve better than a quick fuck. Or a fuck that lasts the entire tour. You deserve something more, Maddie. You deserve someone's love."

"I appreciate that," she says, "but I just want to have some fun on this trip, Jess. I'm not looking to fall in love any more than Dave is."

"Maddie and I are both pretty young," Dave says. "She's twenty-two, and I'm twenty-four—"

I open my mouth, but Dave raises a hand.

"Before you say anything, I know she's the same age as Brianna. But you and Brianna aren't Maddie and me. We're our own people."

One more deep breath. Yeah, not helping.

Maddie rubs her face. "Please just go, Jesse. I promise if I need you, I'll come to you."

"And I shouldn't have to say this," Dave says, "but I promise I won't do anything to hurt her."

"Maybe not intentionally," I say.

"Oh, for Christ's sake." Maddie shakes her head. "Just go."

I turn then and leave the room, closing the door behind me.

I go back to my own room, where Brianna is still asleep.

And I need to release this anxiety.

"Brianna." I nudge her gently.

One of her eyes opens. "Hmm?"

"Turn around. I'm going to force my cock into you."

She moans, turns so her back is toward me, and I nudge my hard cock at her butt cheeks.

Then I slide into her hard.

CHAPTER THIRTY-FOUR

Brianna

To say our walking tour of Glasgow the next morning is awkward is an understatement. Brock and Rory decide not to join us because Brock arranged something special for Rory, but Maddie and Dave are with us, holding hands as we wait for our tour guide to meet us at the agreed-upon location.

She arrives, wearing a plaid skirt and hat with a pom-pom on top. I think it's called a tam. "Good morning, everyone! I'm Lissa. Welcome to our morning tour of Glasgow's most iconic spots. I'm your guide, and I can't wait to show you the city's vibrant history and culture."

I grab Jesse's hand. It's cold, and I force it to warm up on my own. He's not upset, exactly. He told me this morning what he found in Maddie's and my room last night, and though he says he's dealing with it, his body says differently. I'm just glad there isn't a concert tonight. He needs to have a day to be tense. By tomorrow, I'll have worked all the tension out of him.

I hope.

"Our first stop is George Square," Lissa continues, "which is the bustling heart of Glasgow. Take a moment to look around and notice the statues, fountains, and the imposing City Chambers building behind me. This square is a hub of activity and often hosts events and festivals."

The architecture is grand, and once more I think of Diana. Then I think only of Jesse, his hand clamped in mine.

"Try to relax," I whisper. "Enjoy the sights."

He grumbles at me as we walk around the area. Screw him, anyway. I'm going to enjoy the view. I love culture and history, and he won't ruin it for me. I'm tempted to let him stew and join Dave and Maddie, who are talking to another couple on the tour, smiling and laughing. But this is the man I love, and I love his obstinance as well as his other more enjoyable attributes.

We hit the Glasgow Cathedral—a masterpiece of Gothic architecture, according to Lissa. Its soaring ceilings are supported by massive stone columns, and the stained-glass windows depict scenes from Glasgow's history. Still holding Jesse's hand, I listen to Lissa as she explains all the windows in detail.

Jesse finally perks up when we get to the crypt that lies beneath the cathedral. It's dim and eerie, and the stone walls are thick. I rub my arms against the chill, unsure whether it's from the coolness of being underground or the spookiness of the crypt itself.

I look up at the vaulted stone ceilings supported by columns and arches, and my nerves prickle. I almost feel the spirits of the dead.

"This is the oldest surviving part of the cathedral," Lissa informs us. "It contains the tomb of St. Mungo, around which pilgrims have gathered for centuries."

"Who's St. Mungo?" Jesse asks.

I have to stop myself from jerking at his words. It's the first time he's said anything since the tour began.

"He's the patron saint of the city of Glasgow. He was a

HELEN HARDT

sixth-century Christian missionary and bishop in what is now Scotland."

Jesse nods but doesn't inquire anything further. Later I'll ask him why he was so interested in the crypt. The ancient tombstones are fascinating, and once I get over the haunted feeling, I look to my heart's content before we move on.

We hit the Glasgow Necropolis, a Victorian cemetery on a hill, and then Merchant City and Glasgow Green, a historic park by the river.

Then on to Buchanan Street, Glasgow's premier shopping destination, where the tour ends and Lissa leaves us. The lively street is lined with shops, cafés, and restaurants. Jesse pulls me into a pub, where he orders an ale.

"Aren't you hungry?" I ask.

"Not particularly. But order lunch if you want."

"I will. And I'll order for you, too. You have to eat, Jesse. You have a performance tomorrow night."

"God, you sound just like Rory."

"Someone has to make sure you're taken care of," I say.

His gaze softens then, and he squeezes my hand. "I'm sorry."

"Don't be sorry. Just be Jesse."

He chuckles then. "You did *not* just say that."

"Corny, I know. But come on, Jess. It's not the end of the world. Dave is a good guy, and Maddie's an adult. Everything will work out fine."

"I know," he says softly. "I know."

When our server arrives, I order leek and chicken pie for both of us, and an ale for Jesse to help calm him down. Once the food arrives, he dives in.

"Ha! You were hungry."

"Maybe I just like the food."

I shake my head at him. "Tell me," I say. "You only asked one question, and it was about the crypt."

"I found the crypt interesting."

"Why?"

He swallows his bite of pie, takes a drink of ale, and smiles, almost deviously. "I was thinking about pummeling Dave and leaving him in there."

I roll my eyes and swat him. "Get over yourself."

"I didn't do it, did I?"

I just laugh. This is Jesse Pike. He's not perfect, and no matter what he says, I know he'd never harm a fly. He's just Jesse.

The man I love.

CHAPTER THIRTY-FIVE

Jesse

The train ride back to London takes up our afternoon, and this time, Brianna and I sit together. Every time I head to the restroom, I remember our tryst during the long ride from London to Edinburgh. I'd love to relive it, but not with Maddie and Dave sitting across from us on the train.

Oh, hell no.

I'm not giving David Simpson any ideas.

Once we're back at the original hotel, we all head to our rooms. It's been a long day, and tomorrow I have band business all day and the farewell concert that evening.

It's an amazing natural high, being back on the stage where we started this tour.

I lament that Dragon is not with us—some of my anger at him has eased—but he'll be back with the band after this tour.

Since it's our farewell trip to the UK, Jett said it would be okay for Rory and me to say a few words before we start the concert.

We agreed ahead of time not to write anything out but to just be ourselves.

"Ladies first." I motion to Rory.

She steps toward the mic.

The audience is clapping, but not the thundering applause that we've been getting after a performance.

"Hey, London!" Rory shouts into the mic.

The applause grows louder.

"I just want to say thank you. Thank you for welcoming a brand-new band here along with Emerald Phoenix. We've enjoyed being here so much, and we love you all."

Shouts of "Rory!" roar through the audience.

Nice. Some of them were here during our previous concerts.

Rory steps away, and I take the mic.

"Absolutely, sis. You guys have been amazing, and we all love you so much. So on behalf of the rest of the band, my cousin Cage, Jake, Dragon, Derek, and, of course, my beautiful sister Rory, thank you from the bottoms of our hearts for welcoming us to London." I nod to Derek on the drums, and then to Jake, Cage, Rory. I nod three times to begin the count, and they all come in on cue.

And we start to rock.

For that brief time we're onstage, I forget about everything but the music—the melody, the harmony, the rhythm. The synchrony between Rory and me. The beat of the percussion and the notes from the guitar and keyboard.

I get lost.

Lost in the world I love.

★ ★ ★

Our flight to Paris leaves tonight, so we choose not to stay backstage very long. We're all packed and ready to go straight to the airport.

Cage and Jake have gotten over the whole groupie thing after what happened to Dragon. Of course, I haven't yet told them that he admitted to me that the groupies didn't drug him, that he took the drugs himself.

I will keep that between Dragon and me. It's up to Dragon whether he wants to tell the others. I did tell Rory, though, because she and I don't have any secrets. I also told Brianna in confidence before this last UK concert. I don't want any secrets between the two of us either, even though I know she hasn't told me everything about her family.

That will take some time.

David and Maddie are backstage, holding hands. They're talking to Brock and Rory.

I can't help chuckling to myself. Being onstage is a release, and I'm not feeling the tension that I felt when I caught David in Maddie's room.

What a kick it would be if those three damned Steel Rake-a-teers ended up with my three Pike sisters.

What a twist of fate.

I breathe in.

Looks like I have to get used to the Steels whether I like it or not. If Brianna and I stay together—if she's truly feeling what I'm feeling, and we can find a way to be together in spite of our careers—then I'll be with a Steel as well.

I look around, and Brianna has disappeared.

Then I spy her, talking to Zane.

Oh. Hell. No.

I shoot toward them, nearly running.

"Hey, Jesse," Zane says. "I think that's the best you and Rory have sounded since we began the tour."

"Thanks." I drape my arm over Brianna's shoulder.

"I was just apologizing to your lady. I shouldn't have come

on so strong with her and your sister the other night."

He's a little late to the apology game. Jett apologized right away. I'm not sure what I'm supposed to say, so I decide to be frank. "No, you shouldn't have. But I appreciate the apology."

"And I was just telling Zane," Brianna says, "that it wasn't his fault. Maddie and I were both plenty into it at the time, for our own reasons. But all three of us agree that it's best that it didn't happen."

"Absolutely," Zane says, holding out his hand.

I take it and give him a firm shake. My feelings aside, I don't want to make an enemy of Zane Michaels or anyone in Emerald Phoenix. "Thanks. I'll never be able to pay you and the rest of Emerald Phoenix back for what you've done for us. I will always appreciate that."

"Good, man. Because you guys rock, and Jett and I knew that night we heard you and Rory that you were going to make it big. I'm sorry I threatened what will still hopefully be a great friendship by trying to... Well, you know."

"It's over and done," I say.

And with those words, I let it go. It's much easier to let one incident go than a lifetime of envy and resentment of the Steel family.

Zane is Zane. He'll find other groupies to bed. But not my sister and not my woman.

It's probably partially my fault that Brianna was in that situation. And as for Maddie? Maybe she was trying to be something she wasn't. Or maybe she was feeling left out.

I need to be more present for my youngest sister. Let her know that she's just as wonderful as Rory and Callie. Just as beautiful, just as smart, and just as talented.

And God forbid, if she and Dave Simpson end up an item?

He'd better be damn sure to make sure she feels the same way.

"I was actually looking forward to taking the Chunnel to Paris," Brianna says to me as we're waiting outside the venue for the limo that will transport us to the airport.

"Are you kidding me?" I say.

"I know, I know. Emerald Phoenix invited us to share their chartered flight, and you think as a Steel I should be fine with such first-class digs."

"Yeah. I'm the one who shouldn't want to be taking their hospitality."

"You're okay with it?"

I press my lips together and then sigh. "I have to be, Brianna. I have to be willing to accept help when it's offered. It's hard for me, and it probably always will be, but I have to do what's best for the band. When Dragon decided not to come back, to go to rehab, which I admit was the right decision for him, I had to be okay with Brock paying for Derek's services for the rest of the tour. I had to be okay with that because Dragonlock just can't afford it. But we also can't afford to kill this tour."

"So that makes you okay with this plane trip?"

"It takes about a third of the time, and because it's a chartered flight, I don't have to worry about them losing my luggage."

She chuckles at that one.

"Yeah. I know I was an asshole those first few days."

"And just think, Jesse, if you had taken Brock up on his offer to upgrade you in the first place, it probably never would've happened."

"They could've still lost my luggage."

"But they may not have. When you fly first class, your luggage gets priority."

I don't even reply. I didn't know that, of course. Not that it would've changed my mind at the time.

"Whatever," I say. "You ready? Here's the limo."

Emerald Phoenix brings all their own equipment on tour. As the opening act, we didn't have that luxury. We've been renting equipment at each venue. Jake did bring his guitar. But Cage and Dragon—the first night—both said that the keyboard and drums we rented in the UK were better than the instruments we have at home.

I suppose I have to get used to traveling without my guitar. Feels weird being just a vocalist, but Rory and I singing together was what made Emerald Phoenix first take notice of us, so that's the way we will do it from now on.

Brock, Rory, David, and Maddie climb into the limo, and then Brianna and I do.

Of course, Cage and Jake are nowhere to be found. Jeez. They clamber out of the venue, both looking a little haggard.

"Hey, you guys—" Then I stop.

They're here. No reason to give them shit for almost being late.

"What?" Jake darts me a gaze.

"Nothing. So, are you ready to rock Paris?"

"You know it," Jake says. Then he nudges me. "What's with David and Maddie?"

"I'm trying not to think about it," I say back.

We reach the airport, get through security, and head to the gate where the plane is ready.

The plane Emerald Phoenix chartered isn't overly luxurious. But the seating is all wider than a normal plane, and there's only one pilot, one copilot, and one flight attendant.

It's just the band and our guests and significant others.

We get herded on, take our seats, and the flight attendant does her safety spiel. She distributes champagne to anyone who wants it, but Brianna and I just take water.

Ten minutes later, we're taking off.

Once we're airborne, Brianna turns to me and smiles. "I love you, Jesse. I'm so happy to be here with you."

"On such a late flight?" I squeeze her hand.

"On a chartered flight with the man I love. And Emerald Phoenix."

"I love you too."

The air is turbulent, and the plane bounces through the sky. I'm not a frequent flyer, so my knuckles go white around Brianna's hand.

"Easy," she says. "This is normal."

"You don't fly a lot either."

"Not a lot, but I've been on turbulent flights. Going over the Rockies is often like this."

I draw in a breath and let it out slowly. She's no doubt right, but I look across from me to where Brock and Rory are sitting. Rory looks a little green.

"You okay, sis?"

She doesn't reply. Simply nods, her hand clamped onto Brock's.

The air smooths out after a moment, and I breathe a sigh of release.

"See?" Brianna says. "Everything's cool. We're flying over the English Channel, which are some of the roughest waters in the world. The air pressure is probably a mess."

I have no idea if she knows what she's talking about or whether she's making it up as she goes, but her words soothe me. Slightly.

I take the last drink of my water and look for the flight attendant to ask for another. Where is she? Then I see her up front, buckled into her jump seat.

Okay... Not a great sign.

But the air is smooth, until—

My heart drops to my stomach when the plane falls. Or seems to. It's like that feeling when you're on a roller coaster going straight down.

The turbulence begins again, and—

Brianna lets out a frantic scream as the plane rocks and sways.

I'm trapped. My seat belt restrains me. It's tight. So tight.

A drop.

The roller coaster again.

A shrill sound pierces my ears, and the yellow oxygen masks descend.

Brianna is shaking and screaming. I grab the mask, get it on her as quickly as I can.

Then I panic.

The plane drops, and the overhead luggage compartments fly open. Suitcases drop, one barely missing my head.

Time is fucked up.

Seconds fly by, but I see in slow motion. A haze of debris flying around the cabin, clothes tumbling from carry-ons. Vomit from mouths. Screams. Sobs. Shrieks.

I turn to the woman I love, raise my voice above the commotion. "Don't be scared, Brianna. Wherever we're going, we'll be together."

Then I put on my oxygen mask, grab her, and close my eyes.

ACKNOWLEDGMENTS

You know how I love my cliffhangers, and this one is a doozy!

I really loved writing this particular volume of the Steels for a few reasons.

First and foremost, Jesse Pike and his love for Brianna. Jesse is a hero like Talon and Dale—one who loves with a raw passion that isn't always nice and pretty. It's downright animalistic sometimes, but it's also ardent and pure and perfect. I hope you love him as much as I—and Brianna—do.

Second, I cried while writing the story of Ennis and the fire diamond ring. He never loved again after Patty was so cruelly taken from him, so he gave his heirloom ring to his friend Daphne Steel. It found its true owner in Callie Pike.

And third…I've introduced a new pairing—Dave Simpson and Maddie Pike. Encore, the third book in this trilogy, will be a bit different. Maddie and Dave will take center stage, and you'll be surprised where they take us.

Thanks as always to the amazing Waterhouse team—Audrey Bobak, Haley Boudreaux, Jesse Kench, Jon Mac, Amber Maxwell, Michele Hamner Moore, Chrissie Saunders, Scott Saunders, Kurt Vachon, and Meredith Wild.

Thanks also to the women and men of Hardt and Soul. Your endless and unwavering support keeps me going.

To my family and friends, thank you for your encouragement. Special shout out to Dean—aka Mr. Hardt—and to our amazing sons, Eric and Grant. Special thanks to

Eric for helping with *Harmony* before I handed it in to Scott at Waterhouse.

Thank you most of all to my readers. Without you, none of this would be possible. I am grateful every day that I'm able to do what I love—write stories for you!

Peace and Harmony to you all!

MESSAGE FROM HELEN HARDT

Dear Reader,

Thank you for reading *Harmony*. If you want to find out about my current backlist and future releases, please like my Facebook page and join my mailing list. I often do giveaways. If you're a fan and would like to join my street team to help spread the word about my books, please see the web addresses below. I regularly do awesome giveaways for my street team members.

If you enjoyed the story, please take the time to leave a review on a site like Amazon or Goodreads. I welcome all feedback. I wish you all the best!

Helen

Facebook
Facebook.com/HelenHardt

Newsletter
HelenHardt.com/SignUp

Street Team
Facebook.com/Groups/HardtAndSoul

ALSO BY HELEN HARDT